THIS BOOK BELONGS TO

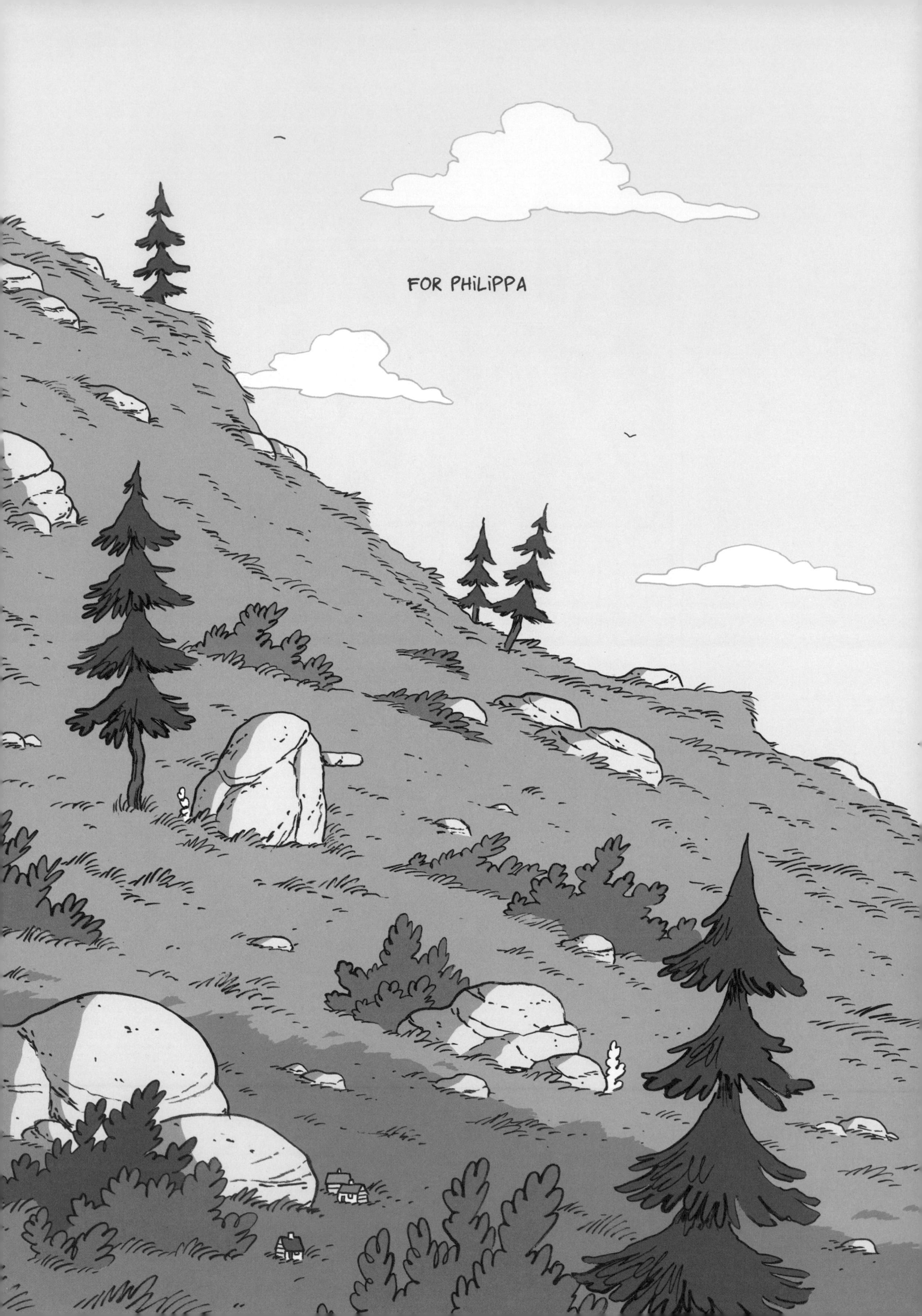
FOR PHILIPPA

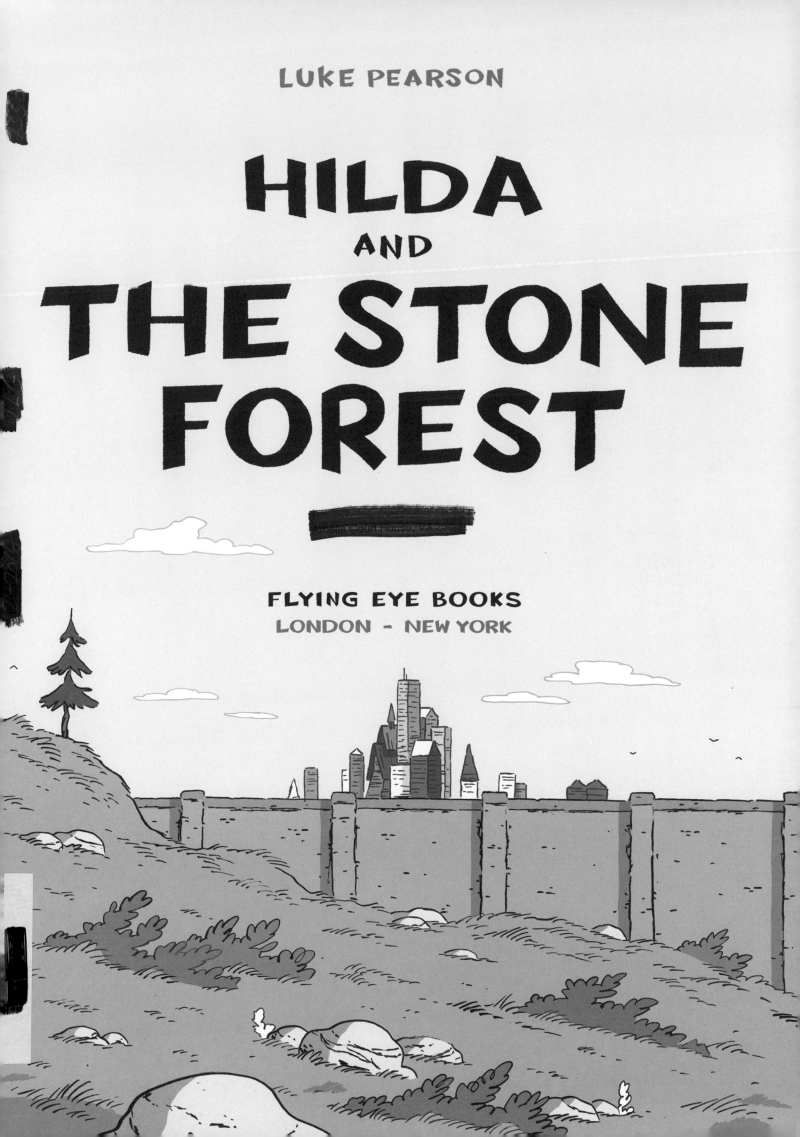

LUKE PEARSON

HILDA AND THE STONE FOREST

[redacted]

FLYING EYE BOOKS
LONDON - NEW YORK

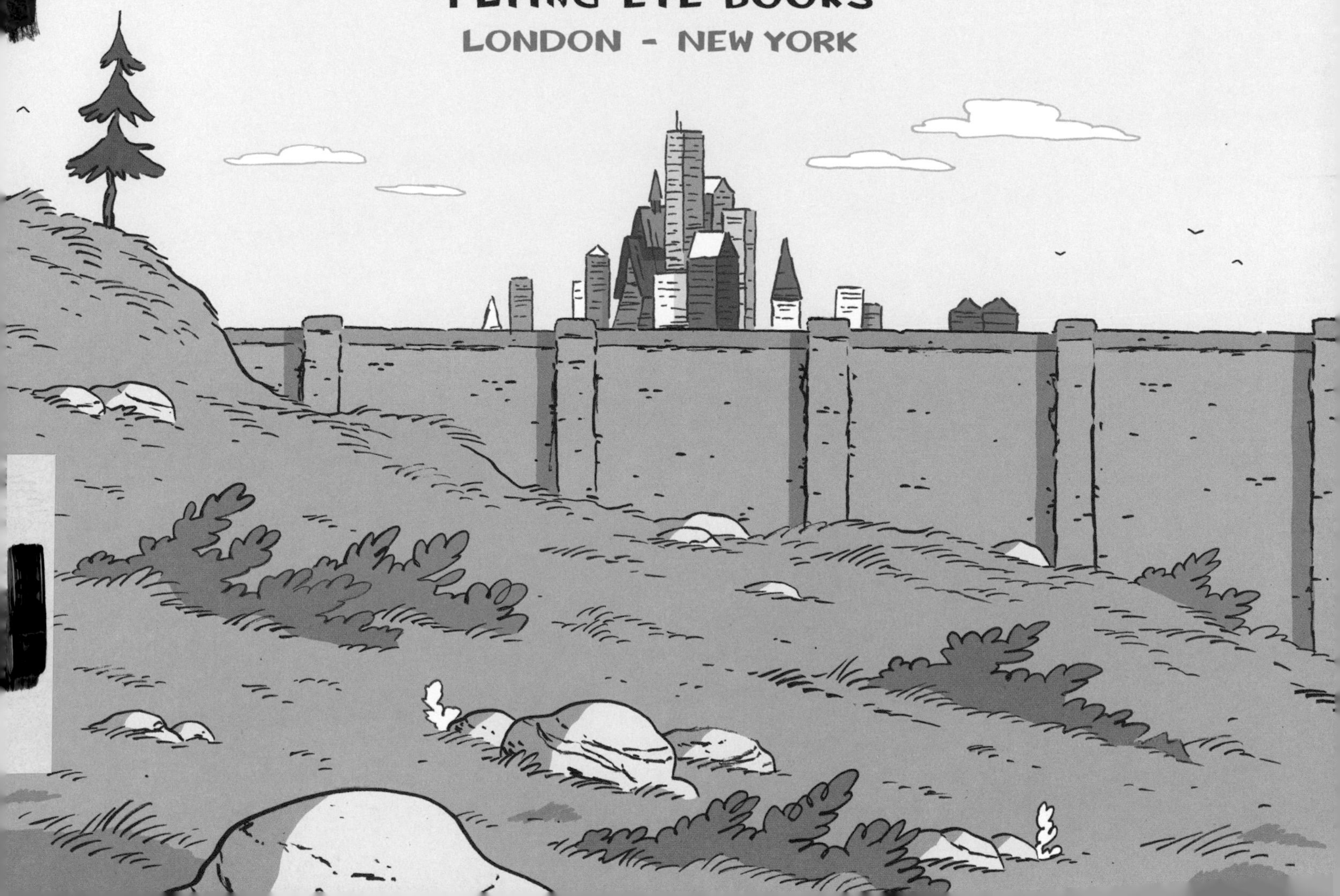

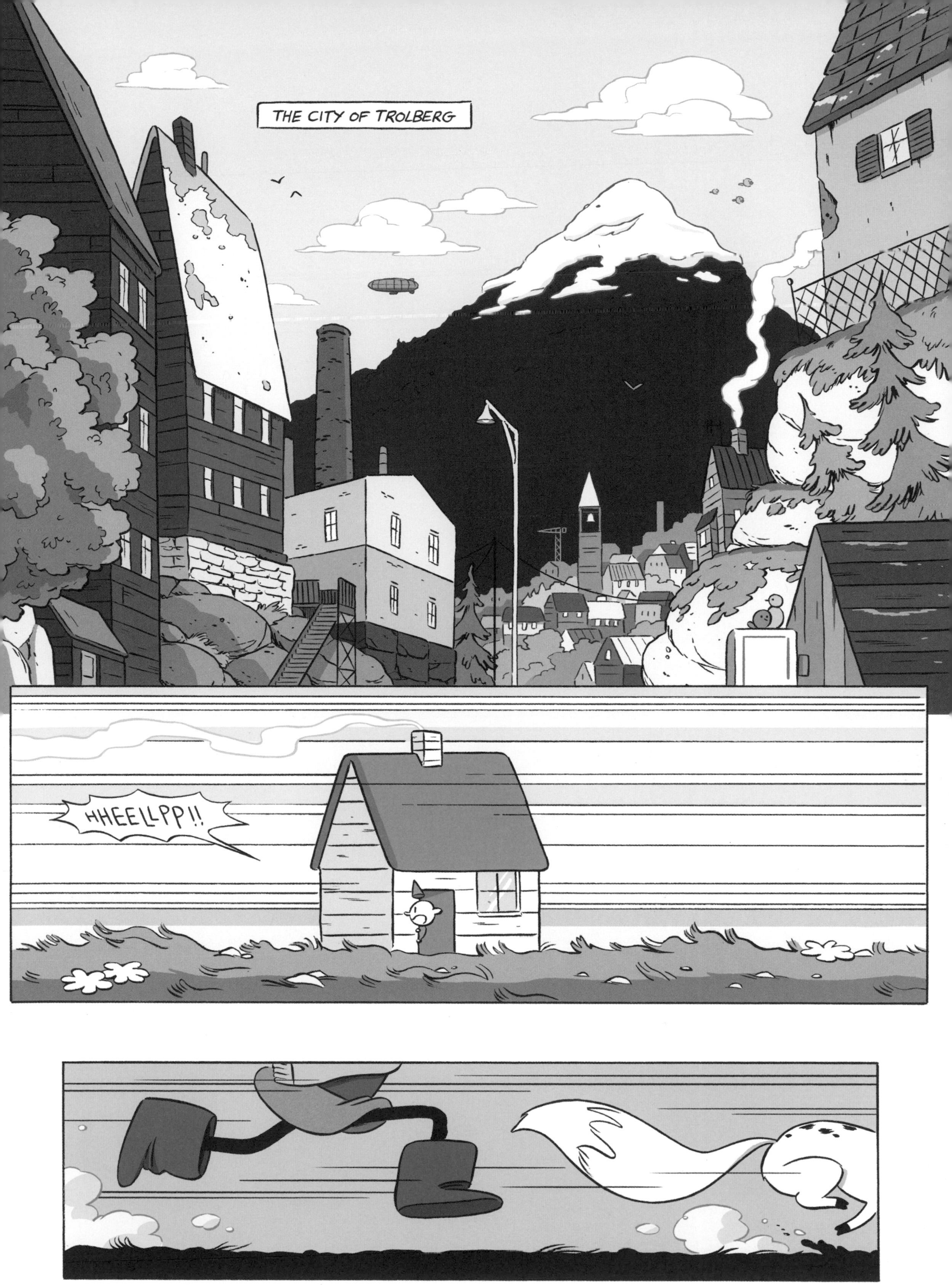
THE CITY OF TROLBERG
HHEELLPP!!

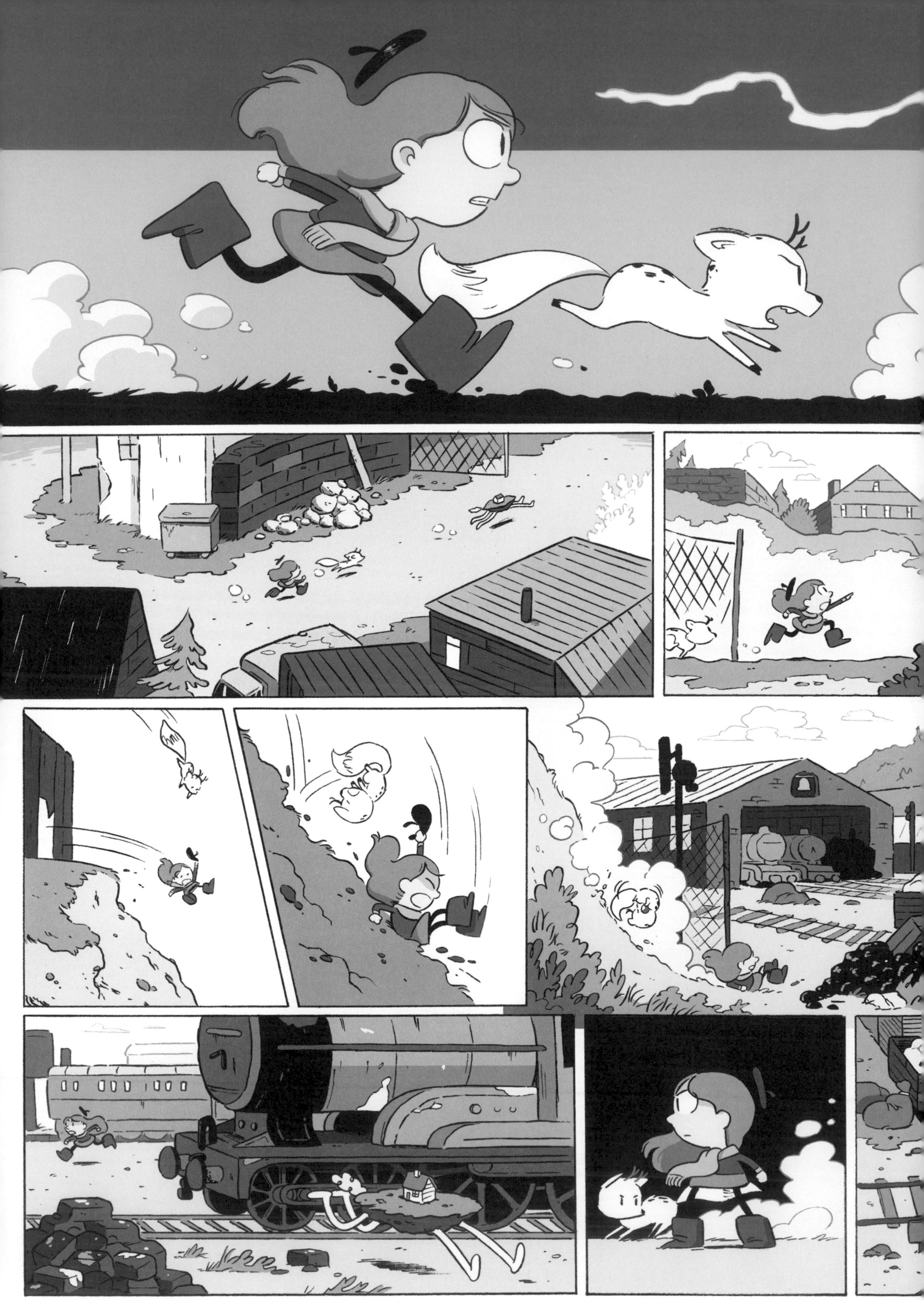

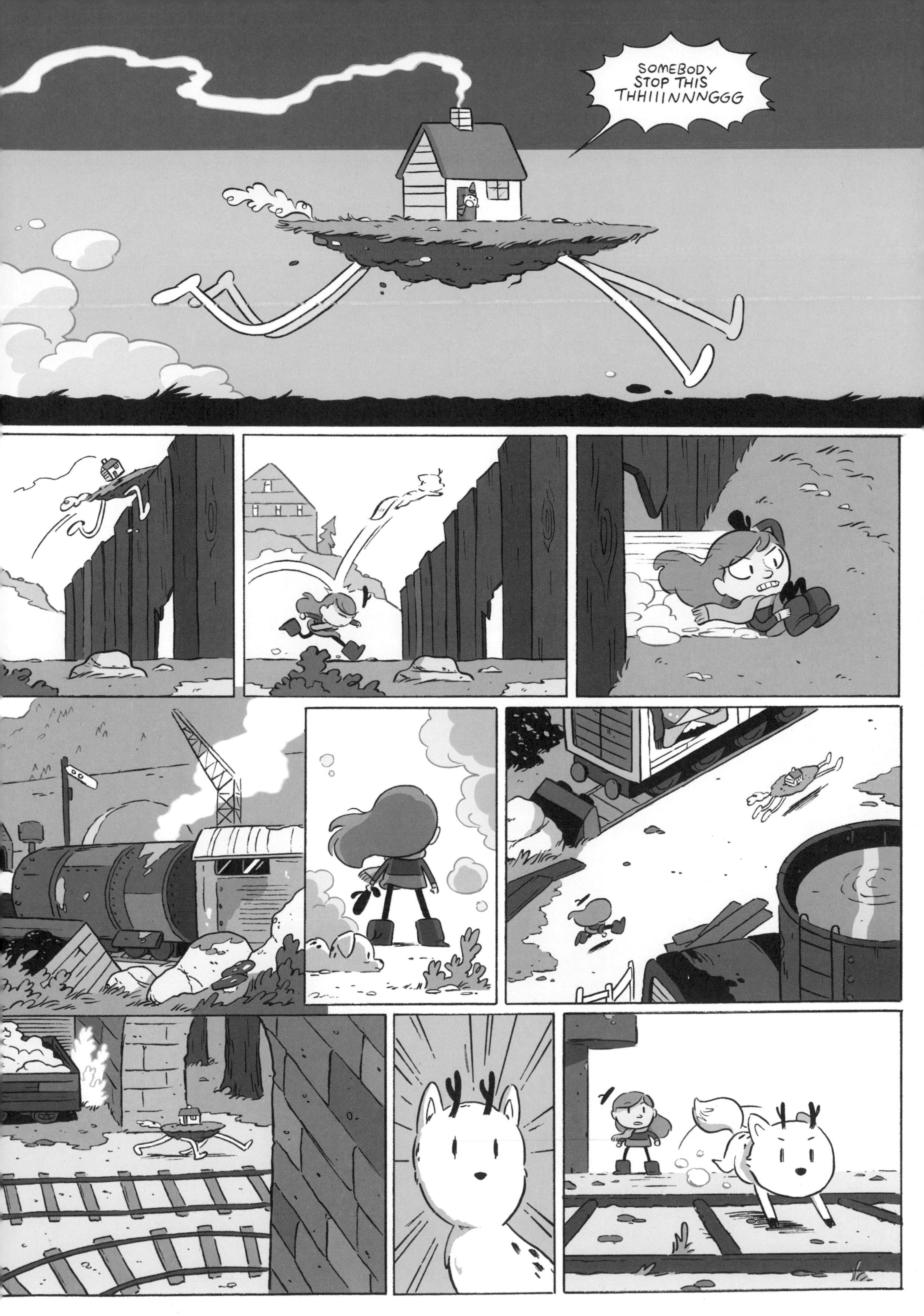
SOMEBODY STOP THIS THHIIINNNGGG

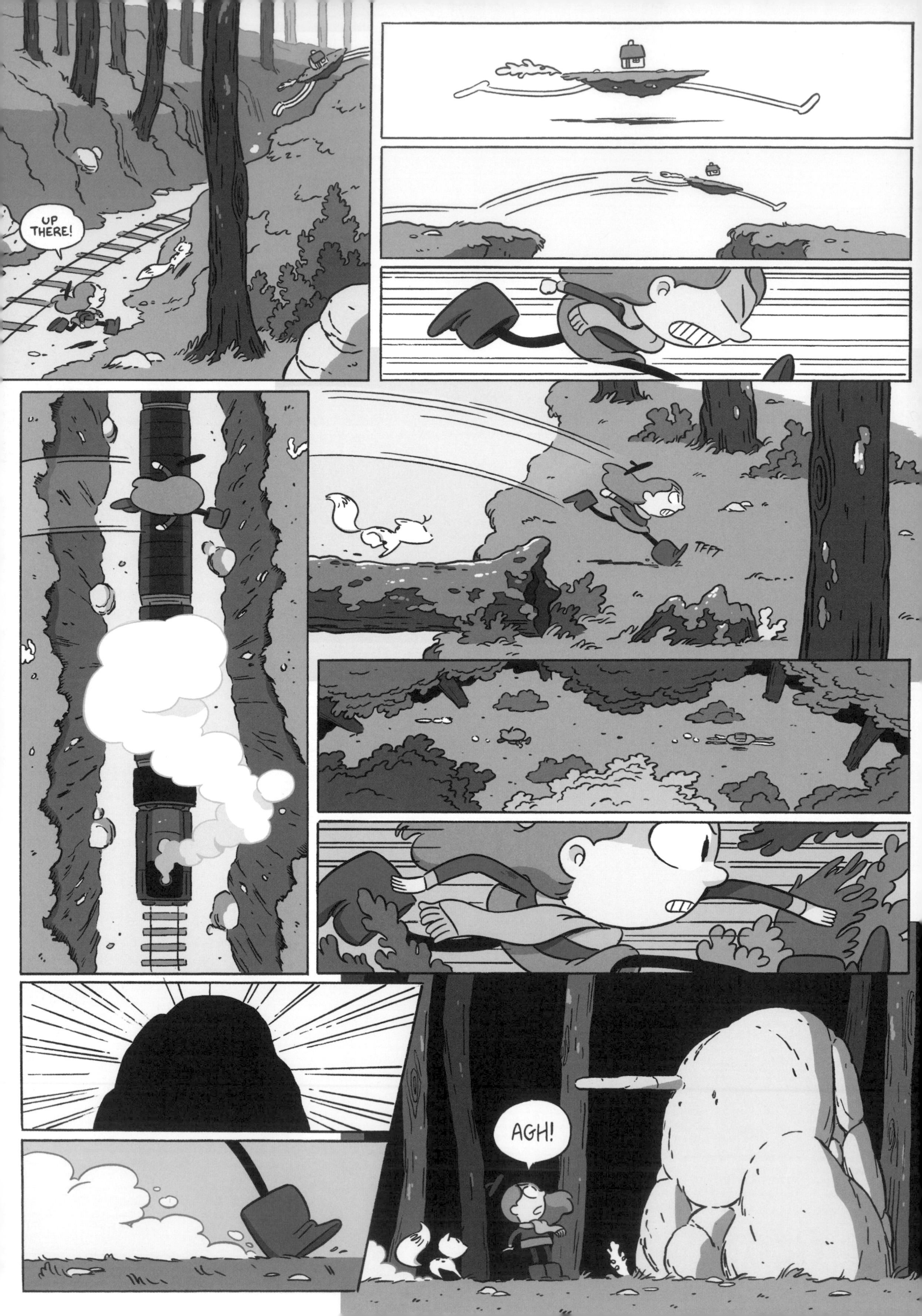
UP THERE!
TFFT
AGH!

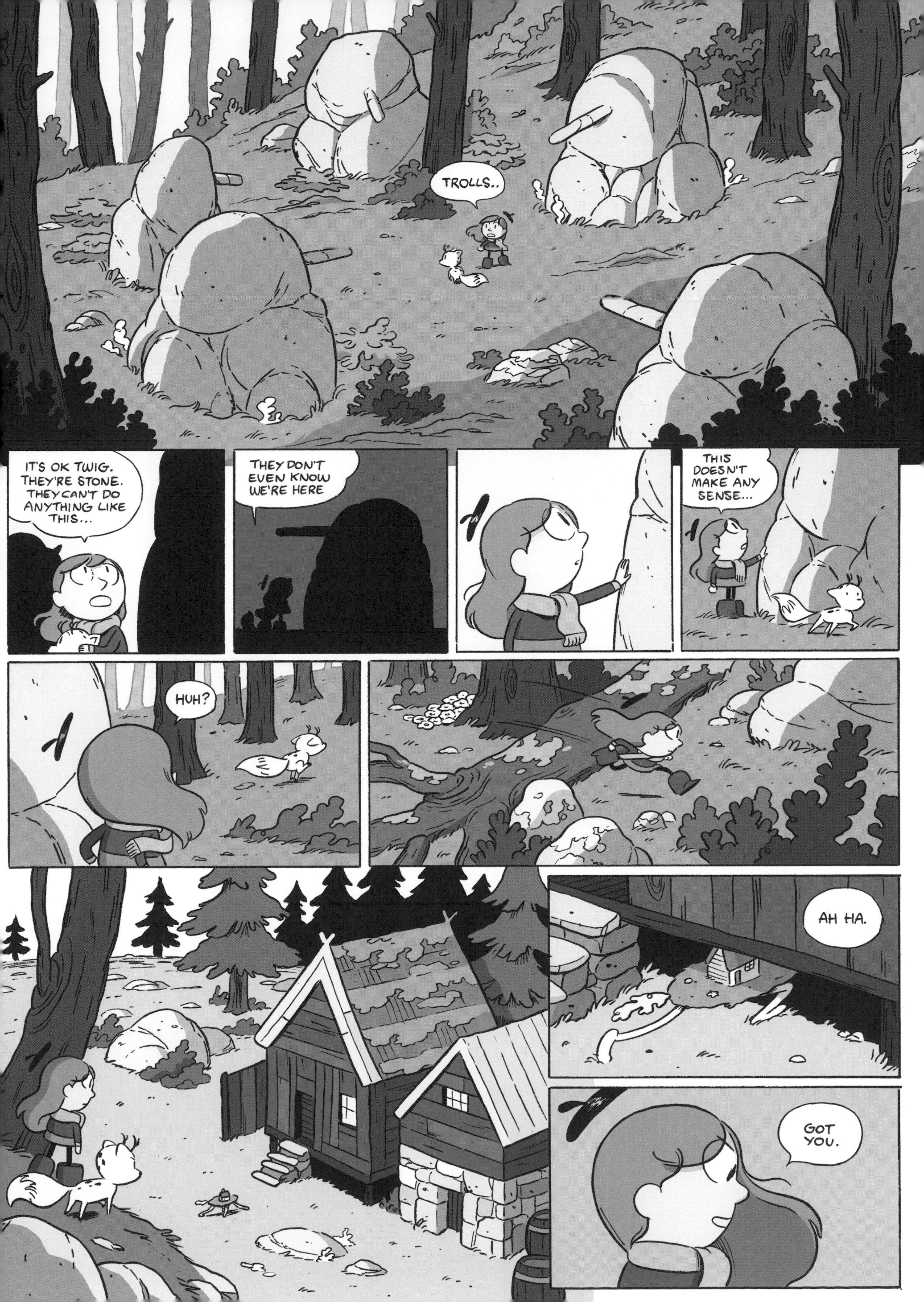
TROLLS..
IT'S OK TWIG. THEY'RE STONE. THEY CAN'T DO ANYTHING LIKE THIS...
THEY DON'T EVEN KNOW WE'RE HERE
THIS DOESN'T MAKE ANY SENSE...
HUH?
AH HA.
GOT YOU.

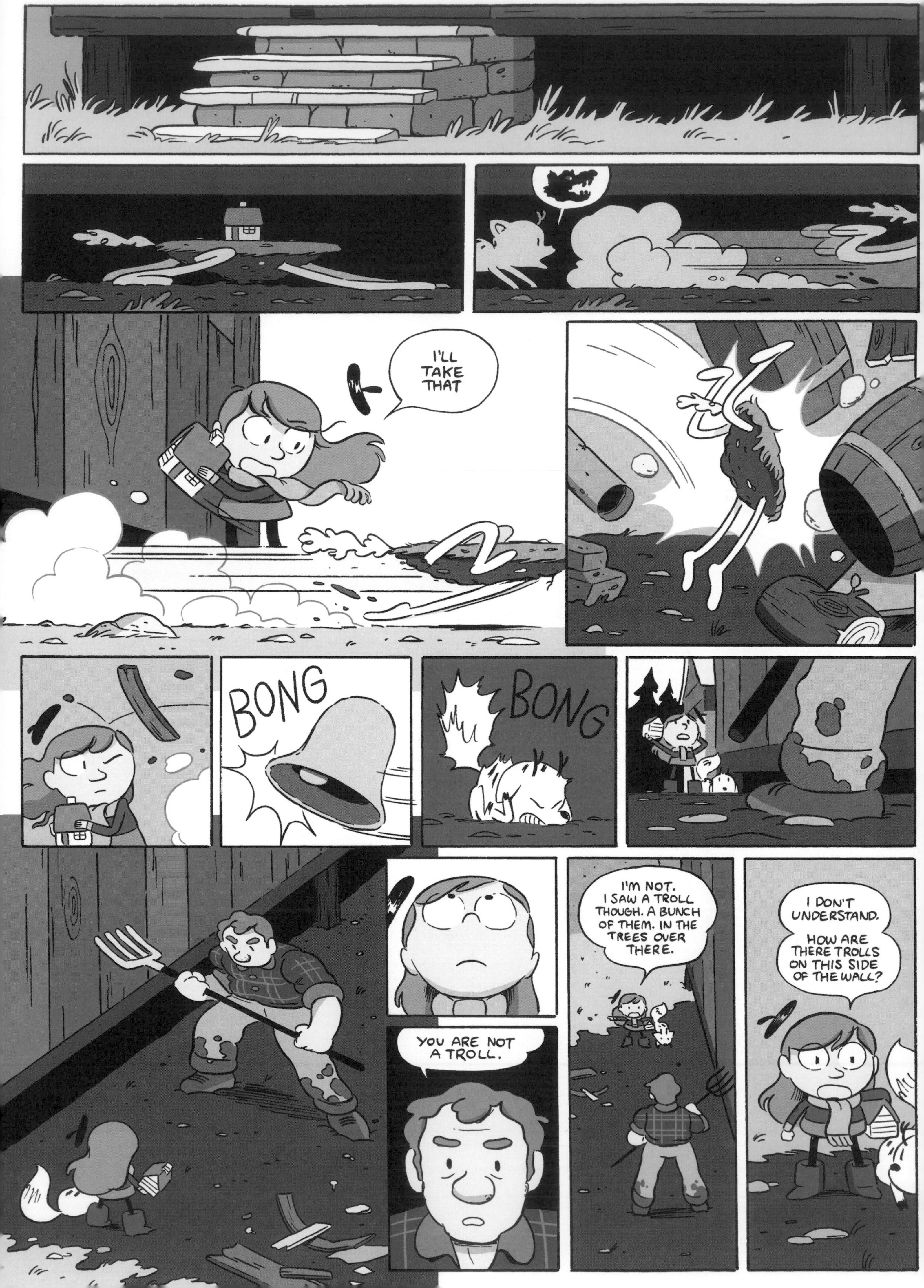

I'LL TAKE THAT
BONG
BONG
YOU ARE NOT A TROLL.
I'M NOT. I SAW A TROLL THOUGH. A BUNCH OF THEM. IN THE TREES OVER THERE.
I DON'T UNDERSTAND.
HOW ARE THERE TROLLS ON THIS SIDE OF THE WALL?

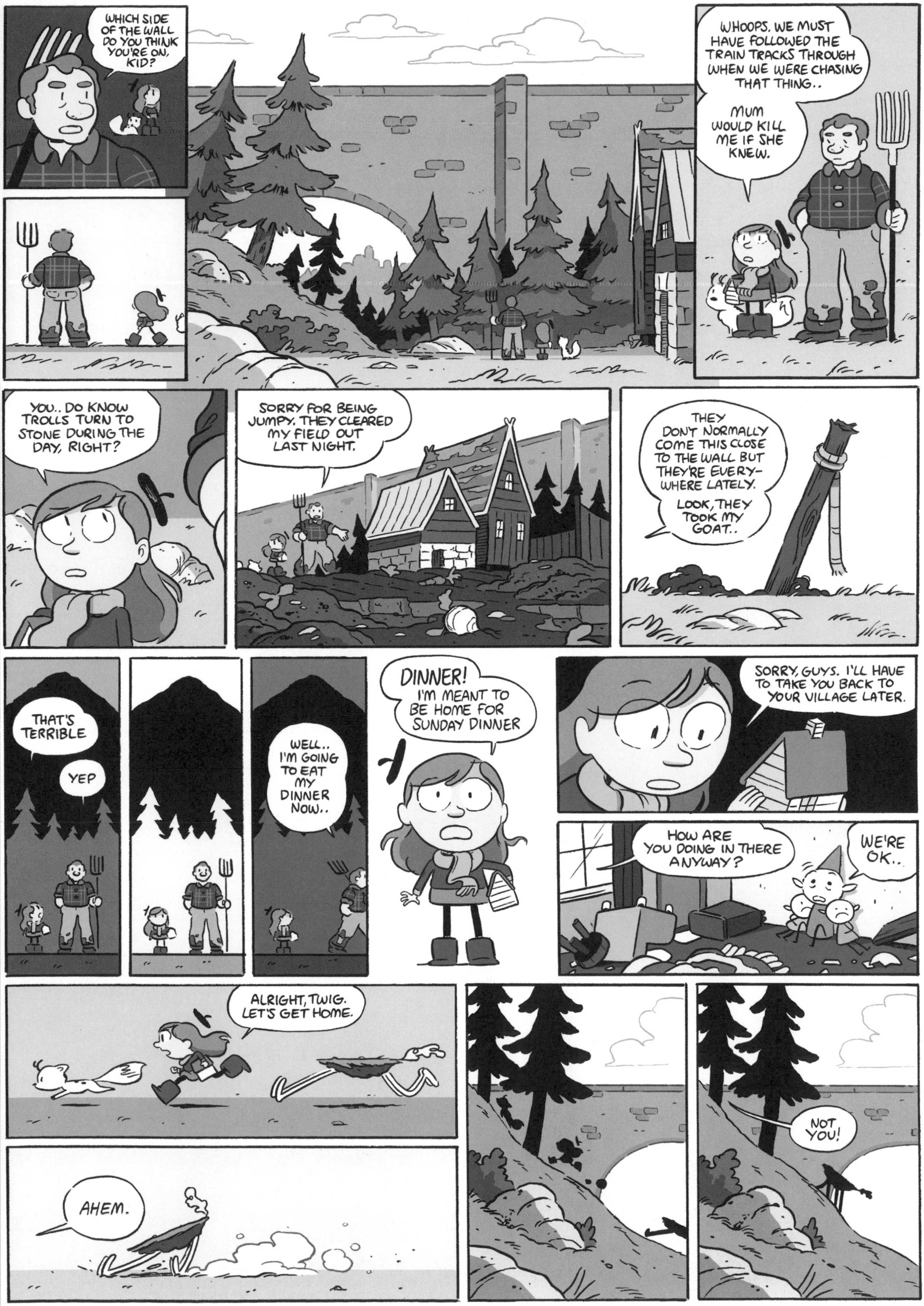
WHICH SIDE OF THE WALL DO YOU THINK YOU'RE ON, KID?
WHOOPS. WE MUST HAVE FOLLOWED THE TRAIN TRACKS THROUGH WHEN WE WERE CHASING THAT THING..
MUM WOULD KILL ME IF SHE KNEW.
YOU.. DO KNOW TROLLS TURN TO STONE DURING THE DAY, RIGHT?
SORRY FOR BEING JUMPY. THEY CLEARED MY FIELD OUT LAST NIGHT.
THEY DON'T NORMALLY COME THIS CLOSE TO THE WALL BUT THEY'RE EVERY-WHERE LATELY.
LOOK, THEY TOOK MY GOAT..
THAT'S TERRIBLE
YEP
WELL.. I'M GOING TO EAT MY DINNER NOW..
DINNER! I'M MEANT TO BE HOME FOR SUNDAY DINNER
SORRY, GUYS. I'LL HAVE TO TAKE YOU BACK TO YOUR VILLAGE LATER.
HOW ARE YOU DOING IN THERE ANYWAY?
WE'RE OK..
ALRIGHT, TWIG. LET'S GET HOME.
AHEM.
NOT YOU!

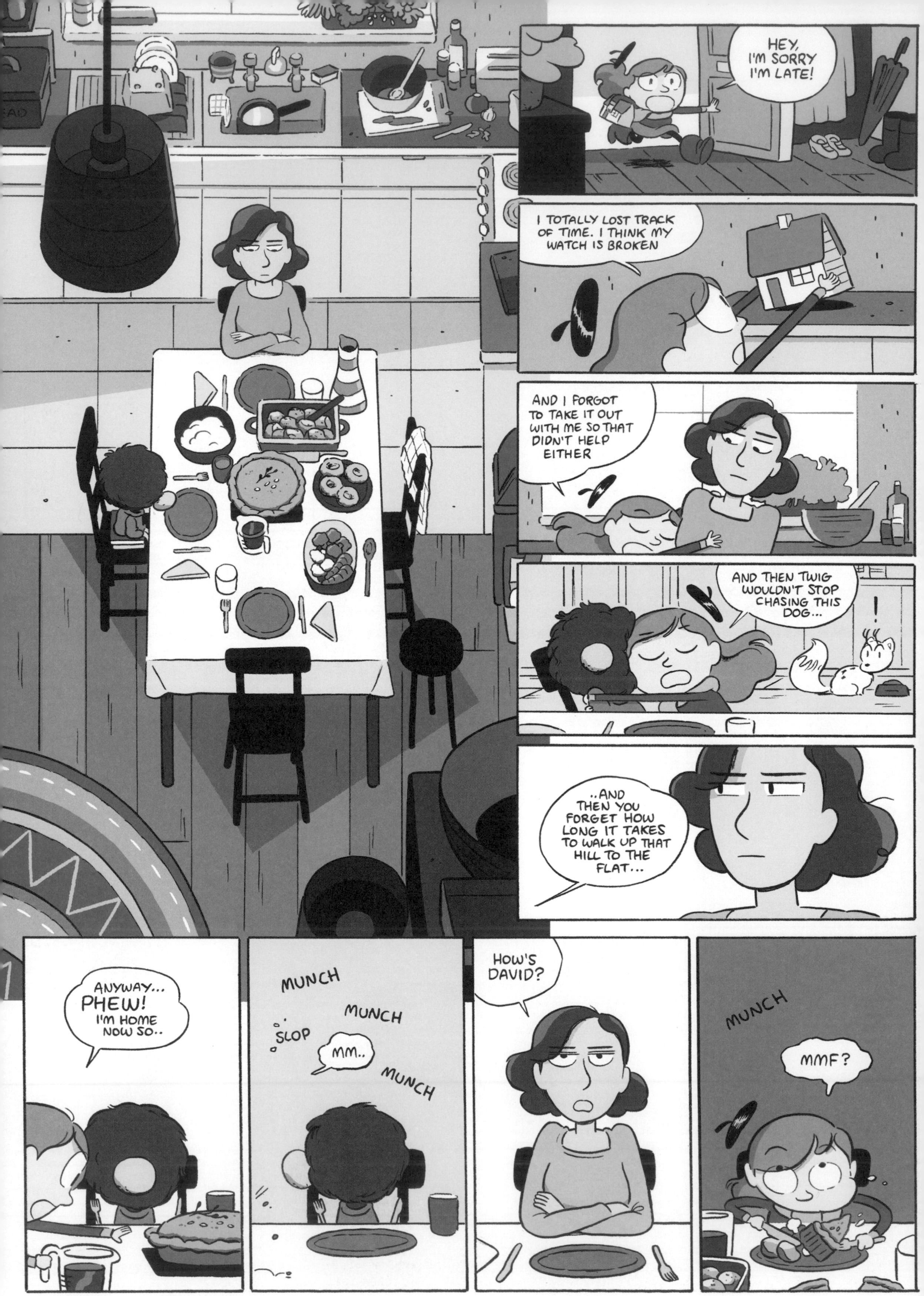

HEY, I'M SORRY I'M LATE!
I TOTALLY LOST TRACK OF TIME. I THINK MY WATCH IS BROKEN
AND I FORGOT TO TAKE IT OUT WITH ME SO THAT DIDN'T HELP EITHER
AND THEN TWIG WOULDN'T STOP CHASING THIS DOG...
!
..AND THEN YOU FORGET HOW LONG IT TAKES TO WALK UP THAT HILL TO THE FLAT...
ANYWAY... PHEW! I'M HOME NOW SO..
MUNCH
MUNCH
SLOP
MM..
MUNCH
HOW'S DAVID?
MUNCH
MMF?

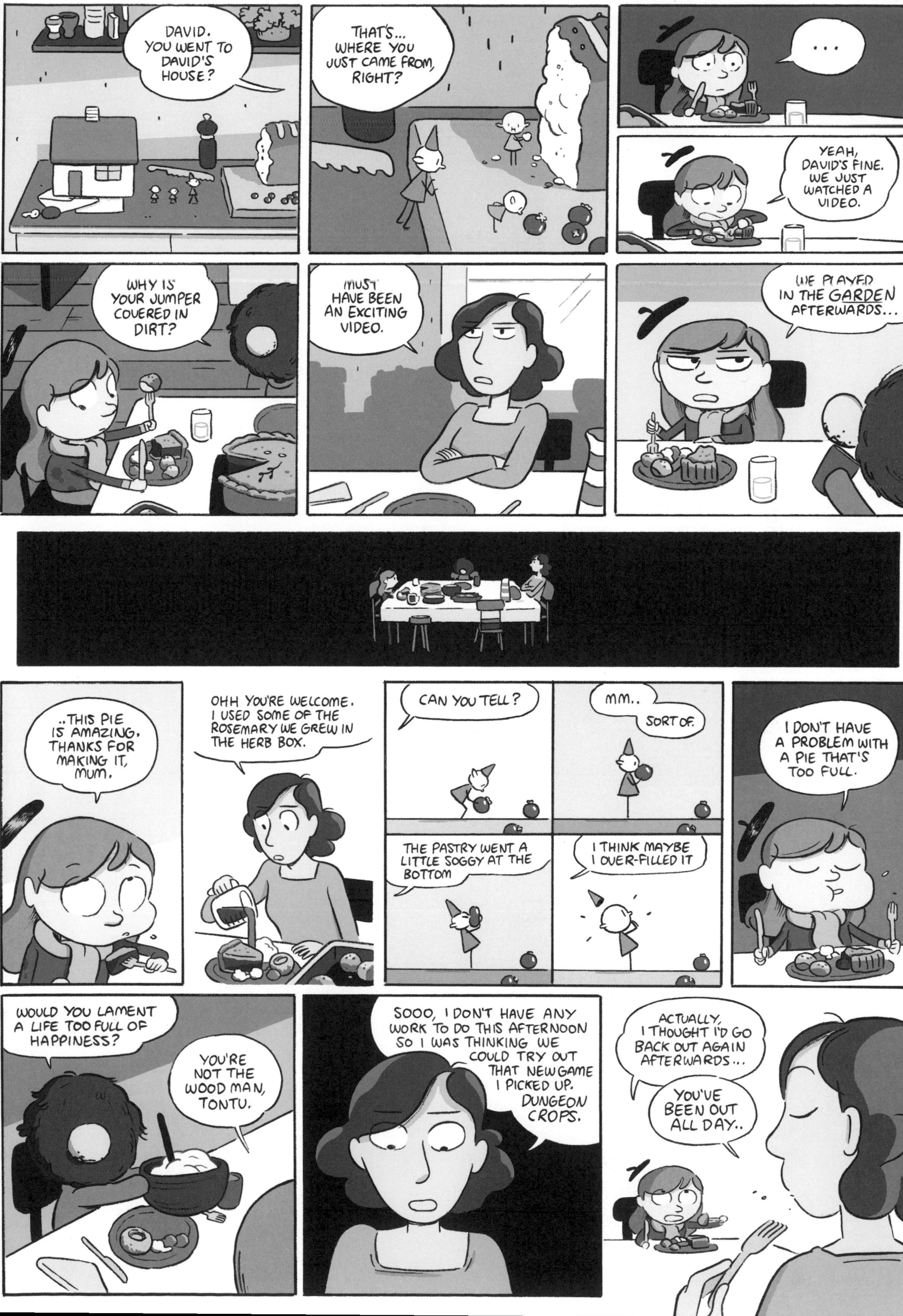
DAVID. YOU WENT TO DAVID'S HOUSE?
THAT'S... WHERE YOU JUST CAME FROM, RIGHT?
...
YEAH, DAVID'S FINE. WE JUST WATCHED A VIDEO.
WHY IS YOUR JUMPER COVERED IN DIRT?
MUST HAVE BEEN AN EXCITING VIDEO.
WE PLAYED IN THE GARDEN AFTERWARDS...
..THIS PIE IS AMAZING. THANKS FOR MAKING IT, MUM.
OHH YOU'RE WELCOME. I USED SOME OF THE ROSEMARY WE GREW IN THE HERB BOX.
CAN YOU TELL?
MM..
SORT OF.
THE PASTRY WENT A LITTLE SOGGY AT THE BOTTOM
I THINK MAYBE I OVER-FILLED IT
I DON'T HAVE A PROBLEM WITH A PIE THAT'S TOO FULL.
WOULD YOU LAMENT A LIFE TOO FULL OF HAPPINESS?
YOU'RE NOT THE WOOD MAN, TONTU.
SOOO, I DON'T HAVE ANY WORK TO DO THIS AFTERNOON SO I WAS THINKING WE COULD TRY OUT THAT NEW GAME I PICKED UP. DUNGEON CROPS.
ACTUALLY, I THOUGHT I'D GO BACK OUT AGAIN AFTERWARDS...
YOU'VE BEEN OUT ALL DAY..

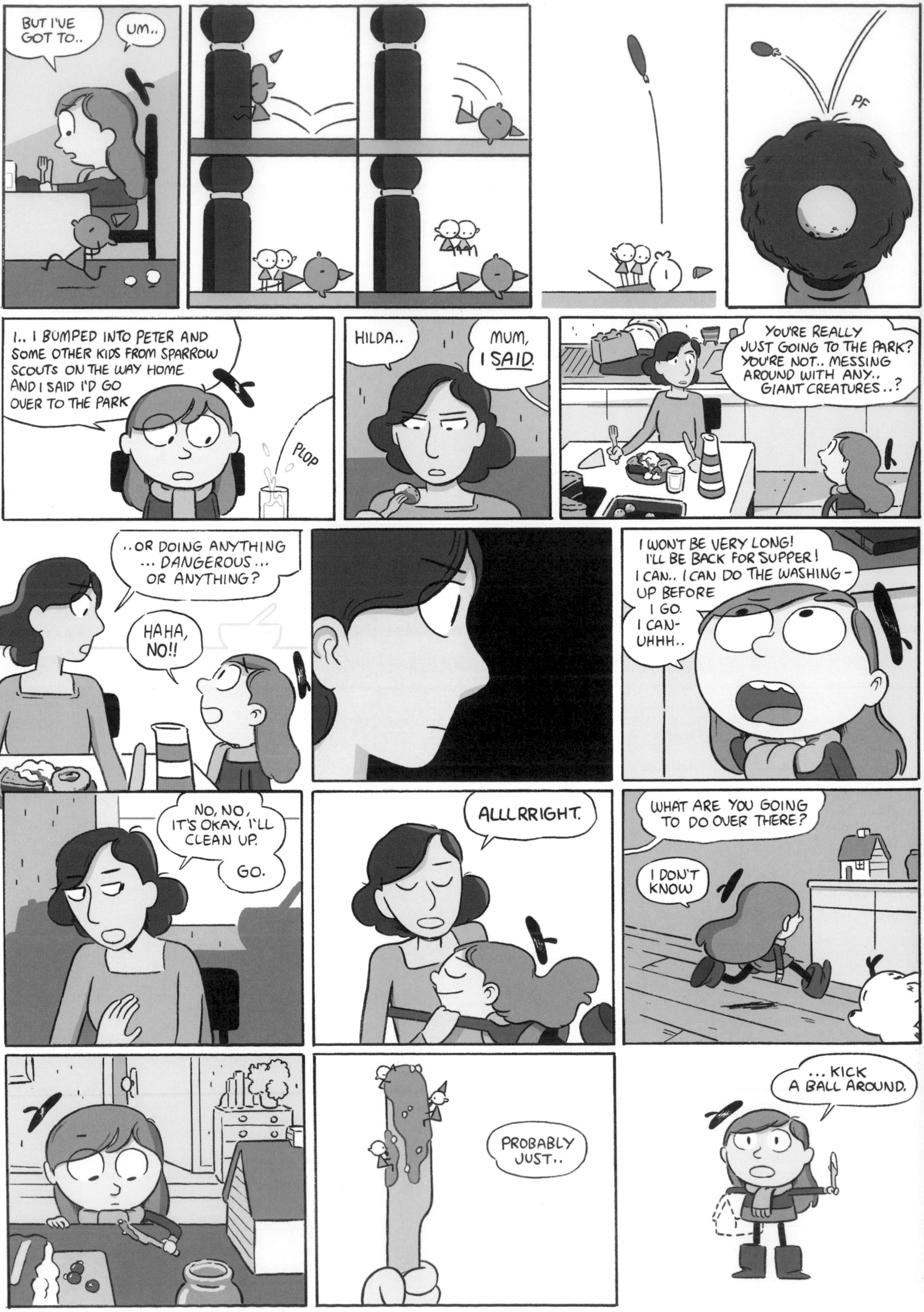
BUT I'VE GOT TO..
UM..
PF
I.. I BUMPED INTO PETER AND SOME OTHER KIDS FROM SPARROW SCOUTS ON THE WAY HOME AND I SAID I'D GO OVER TO THE PARK
PLOP
HILDA..
MUM, I SAID.
YOU'RE REALLY JUST GOING TO THE PARK? YOU'RE NOT.. MESSING AROUND WITH ANY.. GIANT CREATURES..?
..OR DOING ANYTHING ... DANGEROUS... OR ANYTHING?
HAHA, NO!!
I WON'T BE VERY LONG! I'LL BE BACK FOR SUPPER! I CAN.. I CAN DO THE WASHING-UP BEFORE I GO. I CAN- UHHH..
NO, NO, IT'S OKAY. I'LL CLEAN UP.
GO.
ALLLRRIGHT.
WHAT ARE YOU GOING TO DO OVER THERE?
I DON'T KNOW
PROBABLY JUST..
... KICK A BALL AROUND.

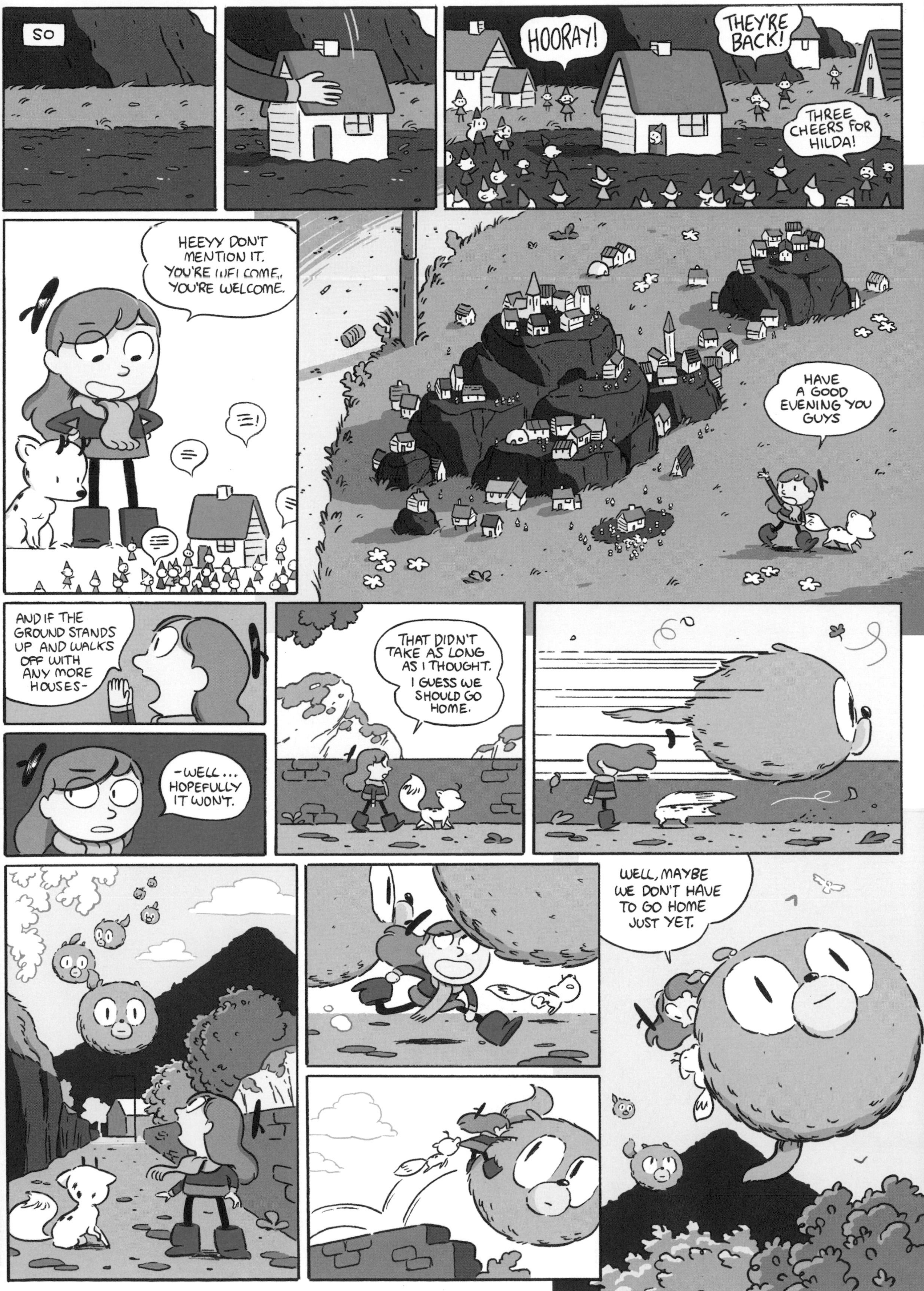

SO
HOORAY!
THEY'RE BACK!
THREE CHEERS FOR HILDA!
HEEYY DON'T MENTION IT. YOU'RE WELCOME. YOU'RE WELCOME.
HAVE A GOOD EVENING YOU GUYS
AND IF THE GROUND STANDS UP AND WALKS OFF WITH ANY MORE HOUSES-
-WELL... HOPEFULLY IT WON'T.
THAT DIDN'T TAKE AS LONG AS I THOUGHT. I GUESS WE SHOULD GO HOME.
WELL, MAYBE WE DON'T HAVE TO GO HOME JUST YET.

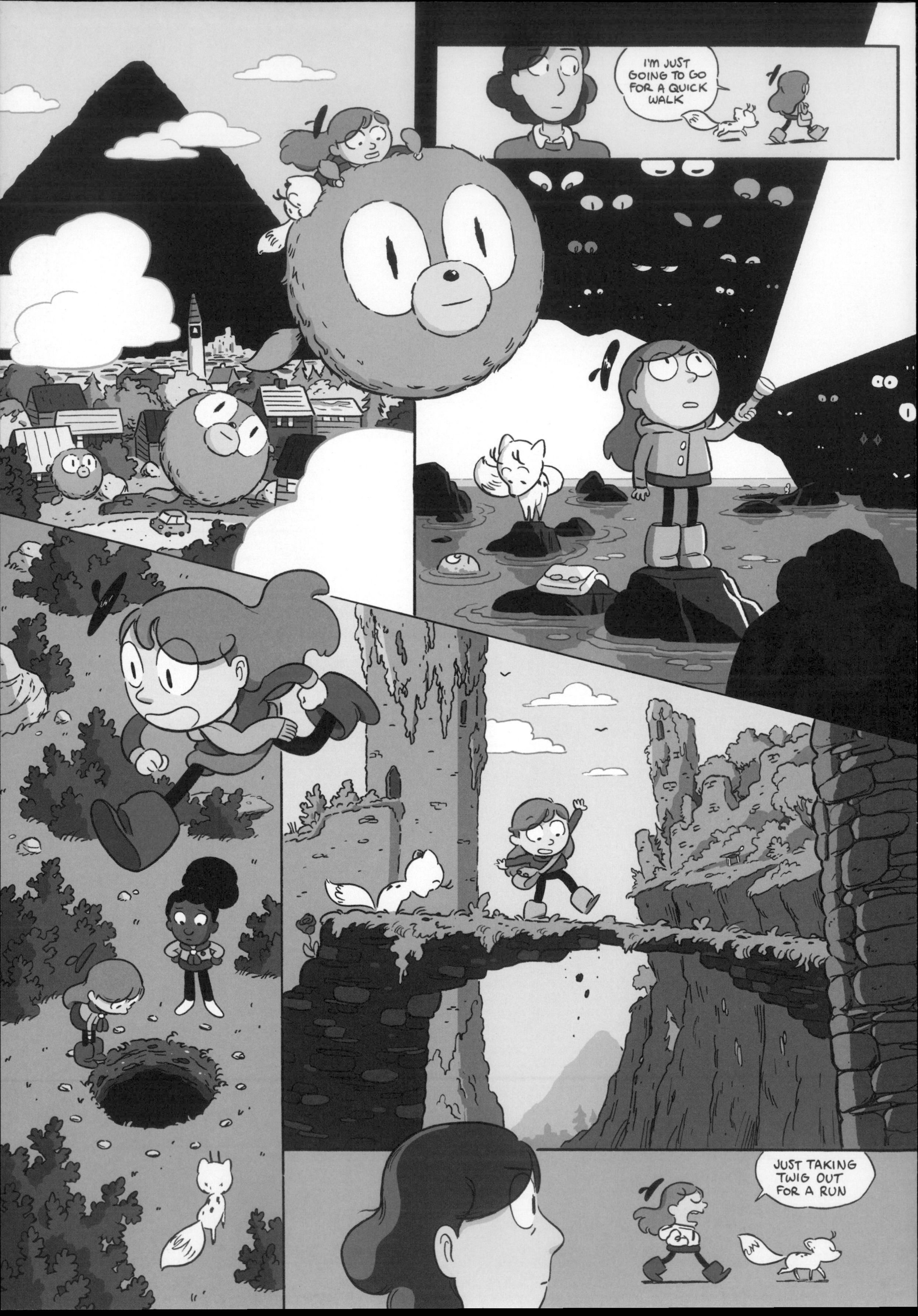
I'M JUST GOING TO GO FOR A QUICK WALK
JUST TAKING TWIG OUT FOR A RUN

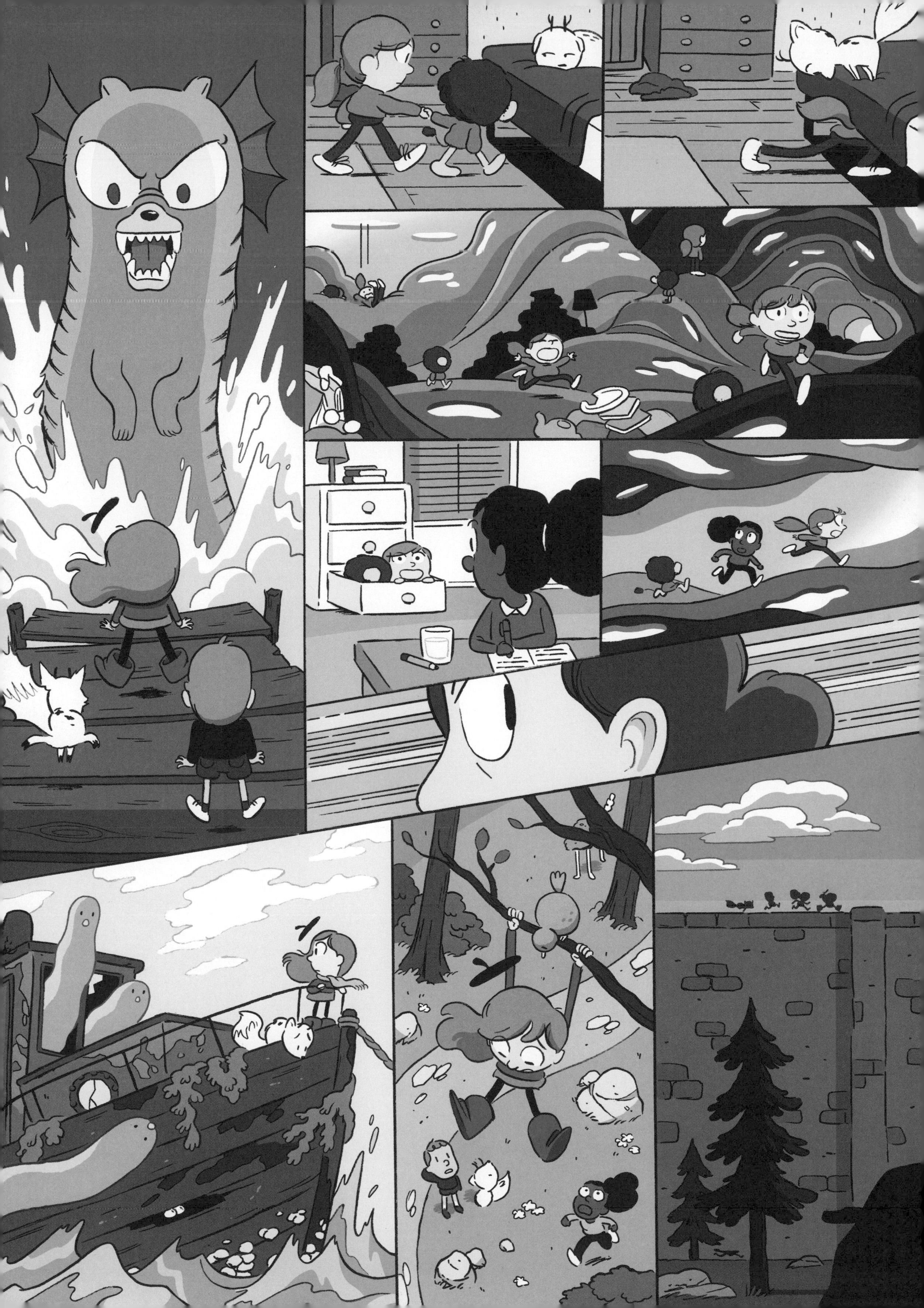

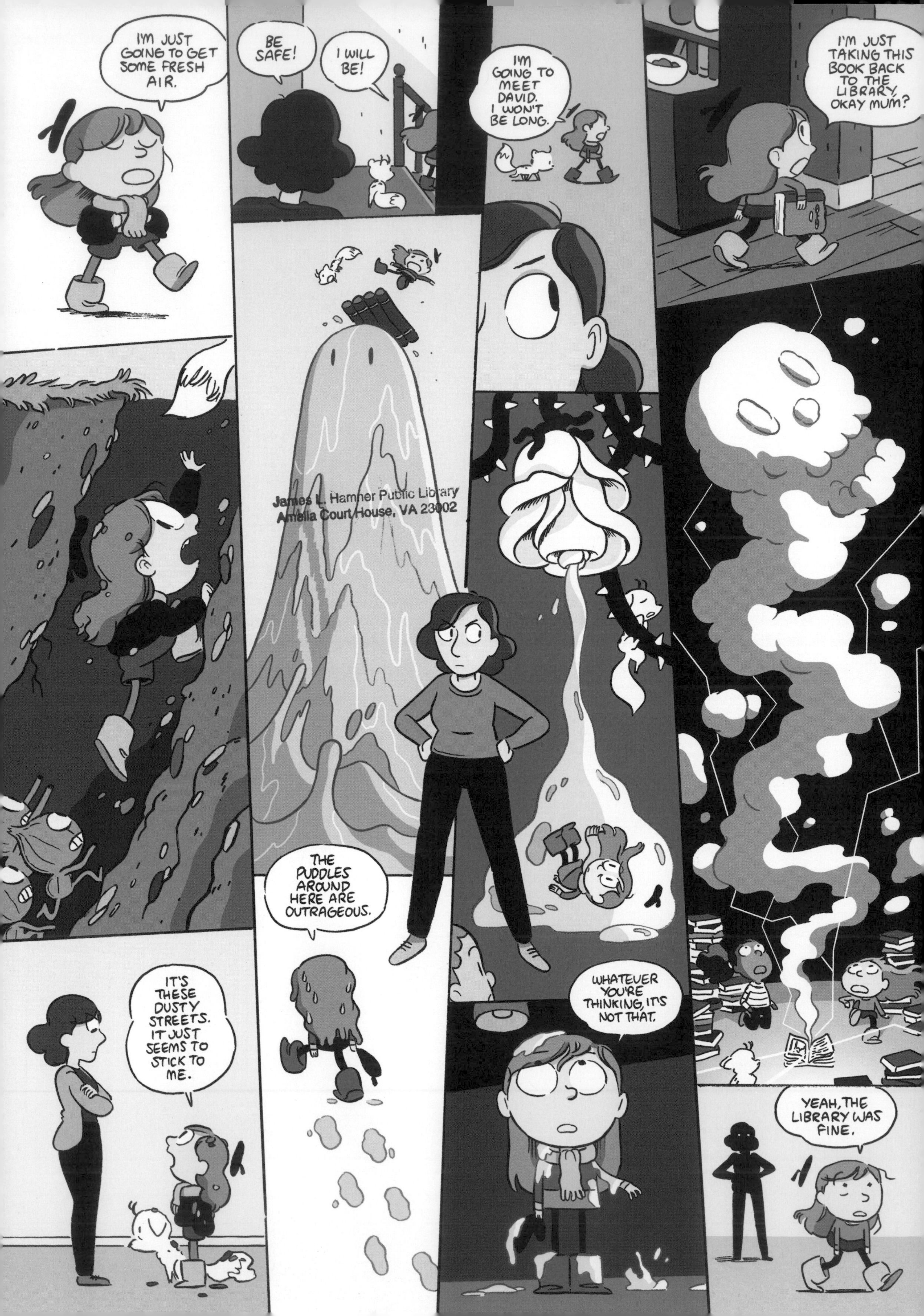
I'M JUST GOING TO GET SOME FRESH AIR.
BE SAFE!
I WILL BE!
I'M GOING TO MEET DAVID. I WON'T BE LONG.
I'M JUST TAKING THIS BOOK BACK TO THE LIBRARY, OKAY MUM?
THE PUDDLES AROUND HERE ARE OUTRAGEOUS.
IT'S THESE DUSTY STREETS. IT JUST SEEMS TO STICK TO ME.
WHATEVER YOU'RE THINKING, IT'S NOT THAT.
YEAH, THE LIBRARY WAS FINE.

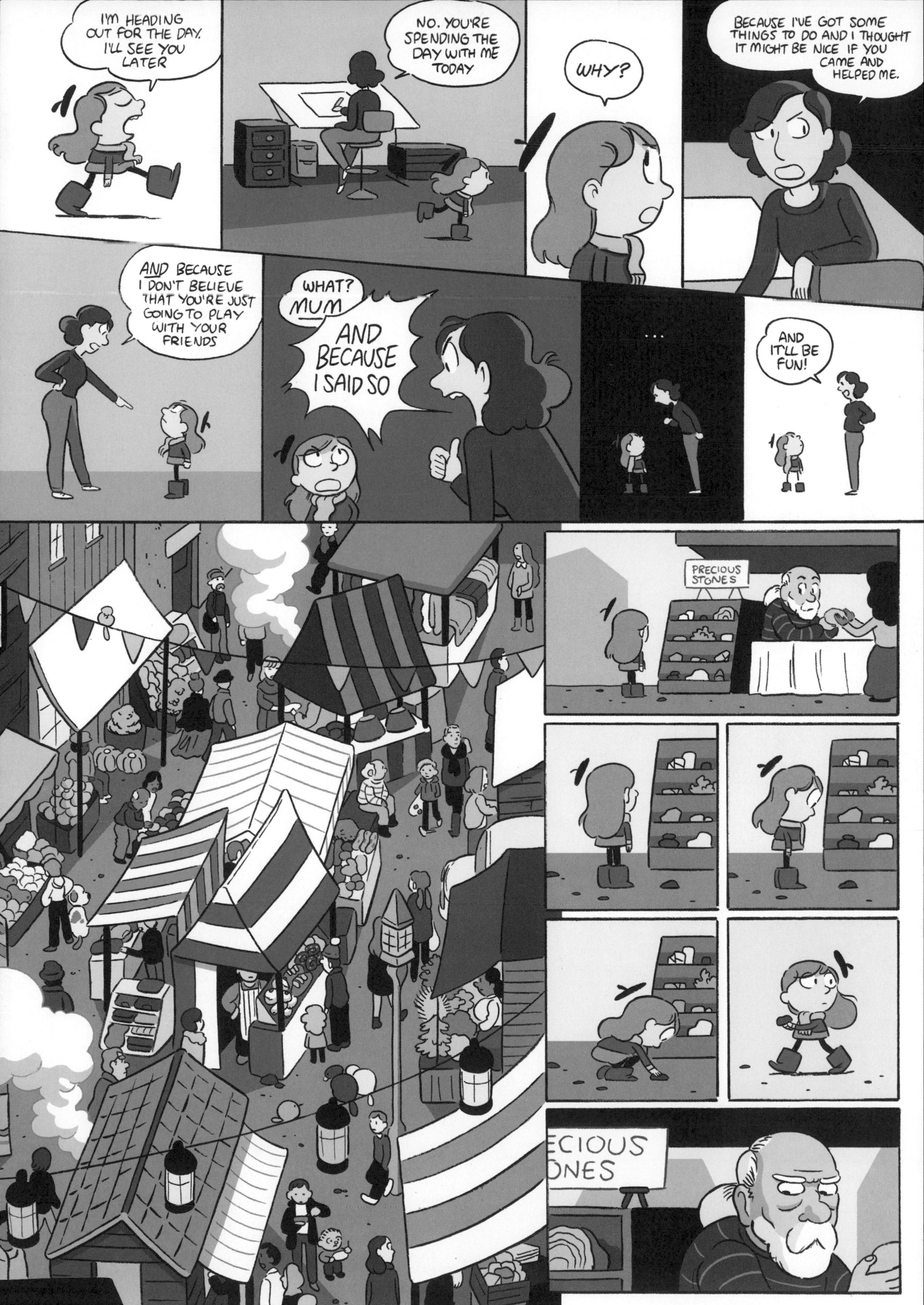
I'M HEADING OUT FOR THE DAY. I'LL SEE YOU LATER
NO. YOU'RE SPENDING THE DAY WITH ME TODAY
WHY?
BECAUSE I'VE GOT SOME THINGS TO DO AND I THOUGHT IT MIGHT BE NICE IF YOU CAME AND HELPED ME.
AND BECAUSE I DON'T BELIEVE THAT YOU'RE JUST GOING TO PLAY WITH YOUR FRIENDS
WHAT? MUM
AND BECAUSE I SAID SO
...
AND IT'LL BE FUN!
PRECIOUS STONES
PRECIOUS
ECIOUS
ONES

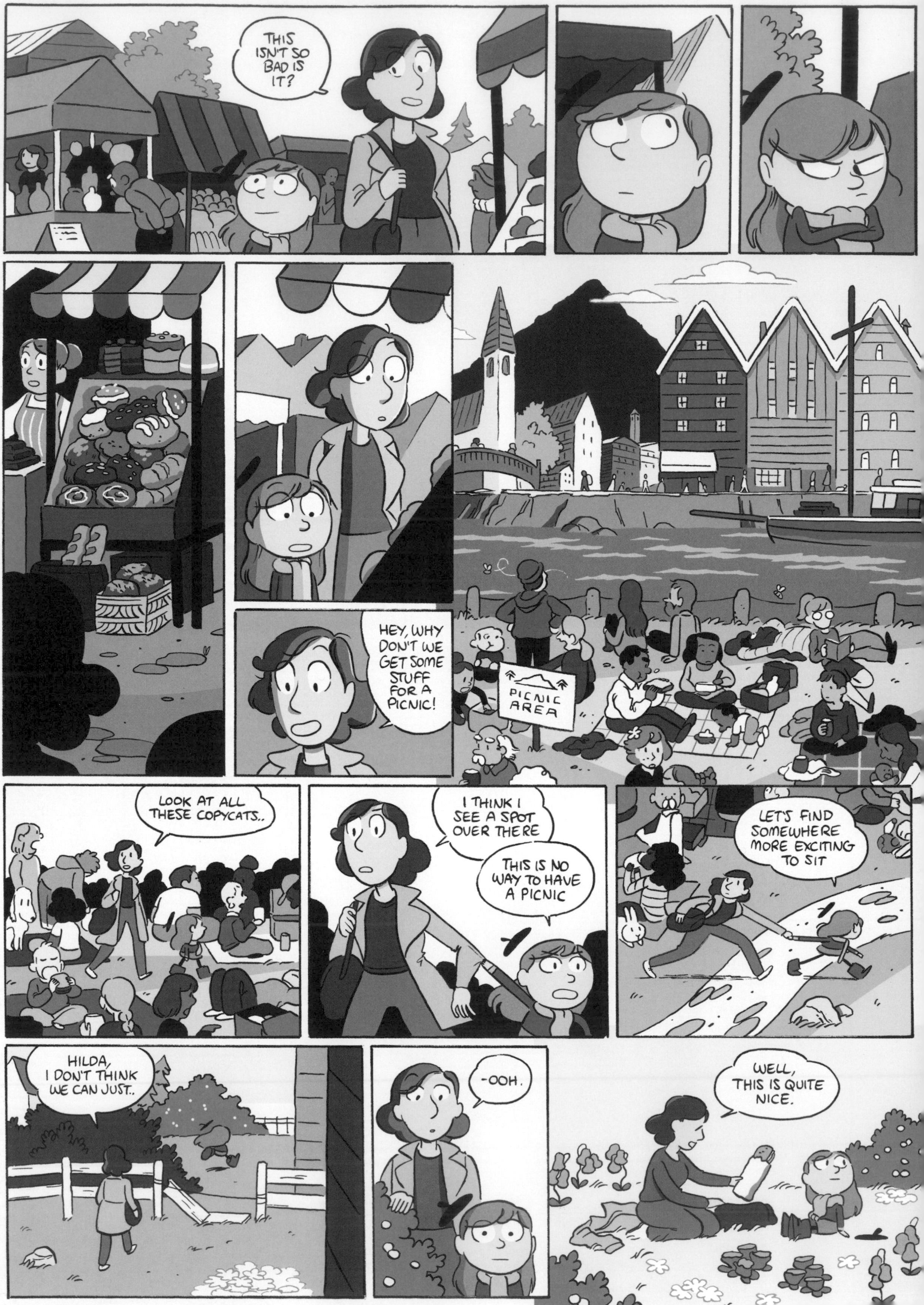
THIS ISN'T SO BAD IS IT?
HEY, WHY DON'T WE GET SOME STUFF FOR A PICNIC!
PICNIC AREA
LOOK AT ALL THESE COPYCATS..
I THINK I SEE A SPOT OVER THERE
THIS IS NO WAY TO HAVE A PICNIC
LET'S FIND SOMEWHERE MORE EXCITING TO SIT
HILDA, I DON'T THINK WE CAN JUST..
-OOH.
WELL, THIS IS QUITE NICE.

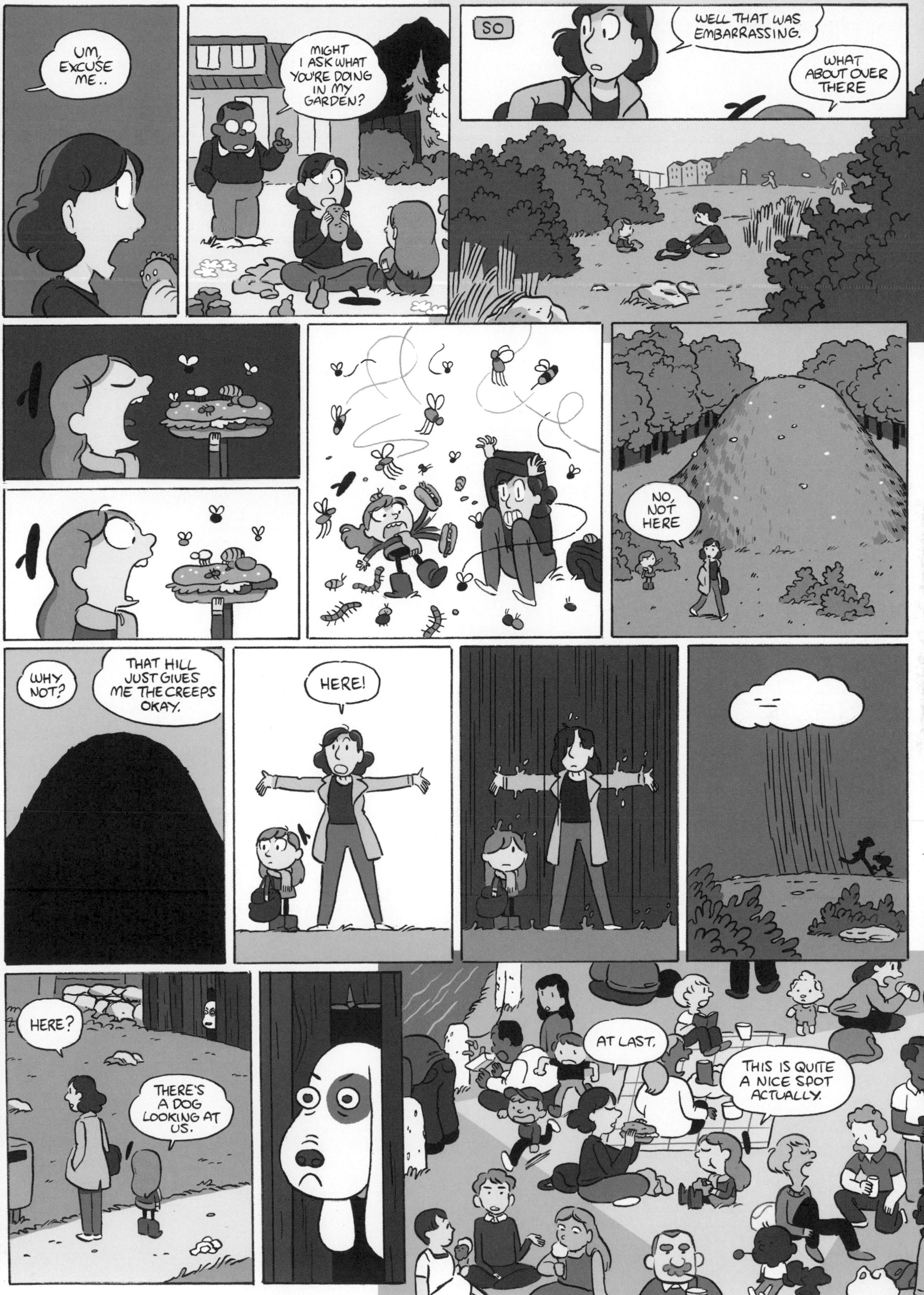
UM, EXCUSE ME..
MIGHT I ASK WHAT YOU'RE DOING IN MY GARDEN?
SO
WELL THAT WAS EMBARRASSING.
WHAT ABOUT OVER THERE
NO, NOT HERE
WHY NOT?
THAT HILL JUST GIVES ME THE CREEPS OKAY.
HERE!
HERE?
THERE'S A DOG LOOKING AT US.
AT LAST.
THIS IS QUITE A NICE SPOT ACTUALLY.

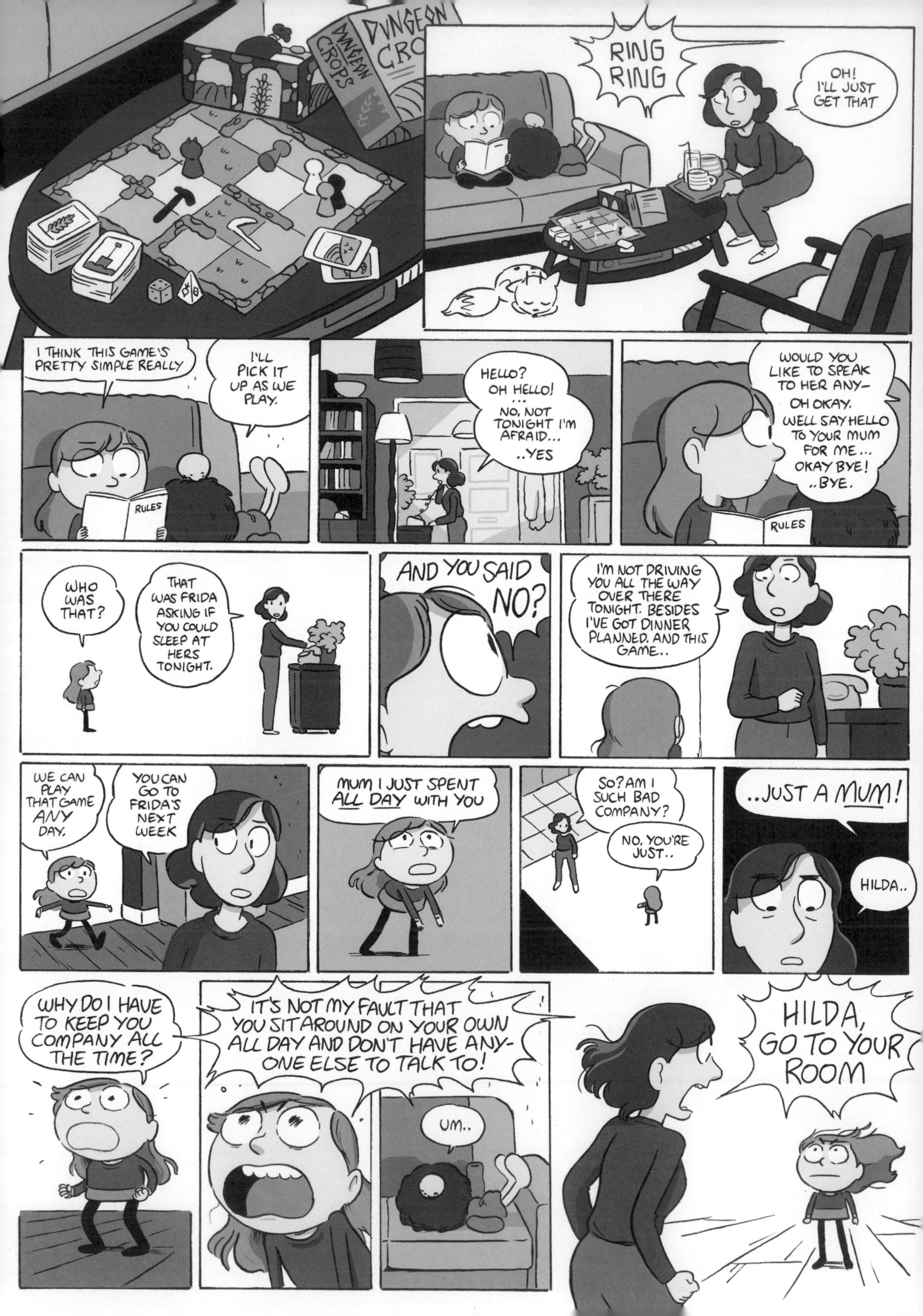
DUNGEON CROPS
DUNGEON CROPS
RING RING
OH! I'LL JUST GET THAT
I THINK THIS GAME'S PRETTY SIMPLE REALLY
I'LL PICK IT UP AS WE PLAY.
RULES
HELLO? OH HELLO! ... NO, NOT TONIGHT I'M AFRAID... ..YES
WOULD YOU LIKE TO SPEAK TO HER ANY- OH OKAY. WELL SAY HELLO TO YOUR MUM FOR ME... OKAY BYE! ..BYE.
RULES
WHO WAS THAT?
THAT WAS FRIDA ASKING IF YOU COULD SLEEP AT HERS TONIGHT.
AND YOU SAID NO?
I'M NOT DRIVING YOU ALL THE WAY OVER THERE TONIGHT. BESIDES I'VE GOT DINNER PLANNED. AND THIS GAME..
WE CAN PLAY THAT GAME ANY DAY.
YOU CAN GO TO FRIDA'S NEXT WEEK
MUM I JUST SPENT ALL DAY WITH YOU
SO? AM I SUCH BAD COMPANY?
NO, YOU'RE JUST..
..JUST A MUM!
HILDA..
WHY DO I HAVE TO KEEP YOU COMPANY ALL THE TIME?
IT'S NOT MY FAULT THAT YOU SIT AROUND ON YOUR OWN ALL DAY AND DON'T HAVE ANYONE ELSE TO TALK TO!
UM..
HILDA, GO TO YOUR ROOM

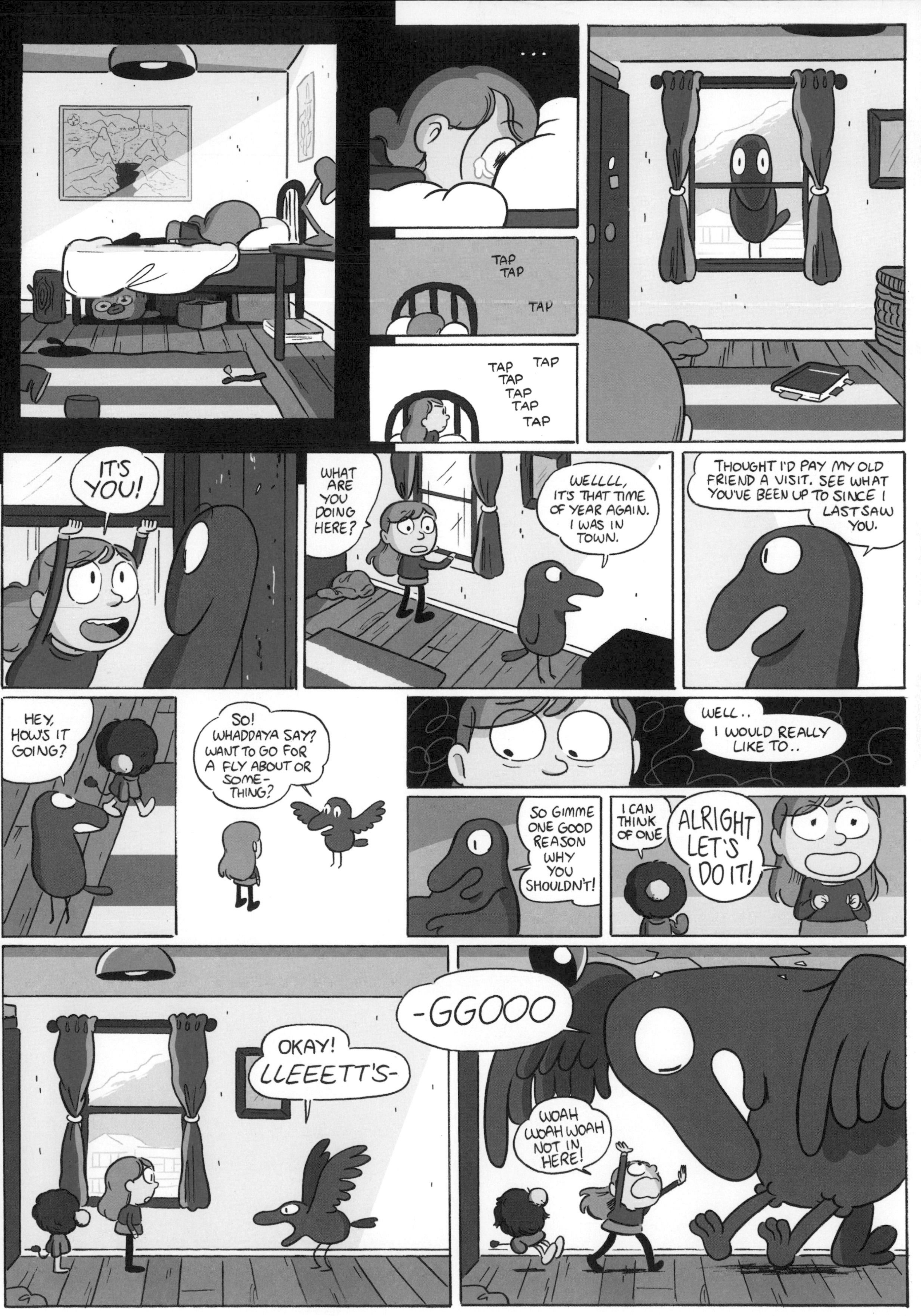
...
TAP
TAP
TAP
TAP TAP
TAP
TAP
TAP
TAP
IT'S YOU!
WHAT ARE YOU DOING HERE?
WELLLL, IT'S THAT TIME OF YEAR AGAIN. I WAS IN TOWN.
THOUGHT I'D PAY MY OLD FRIEND A VISIT. SEE WHAT YOU'VE BEEN UP TO SINCE I LAST SAW YOU.
HEY, HOW'S IT GOING?
SO! WHADDAYA SAY? WANT TO GO FOR A FLY ABOUT OR SOME-THING?
WELL.. I WOULD REALLY LIKE TO..
SO GIMME ONE GOOD REASON WHY YOU SHOULDN'T!
I CAN THINK OF ONE
ALRIGHT LET'S DO IT!
OKAY! LLEEETT'S-
-GGOOO
WOAH WOAH WOAH NOT IN HERE!

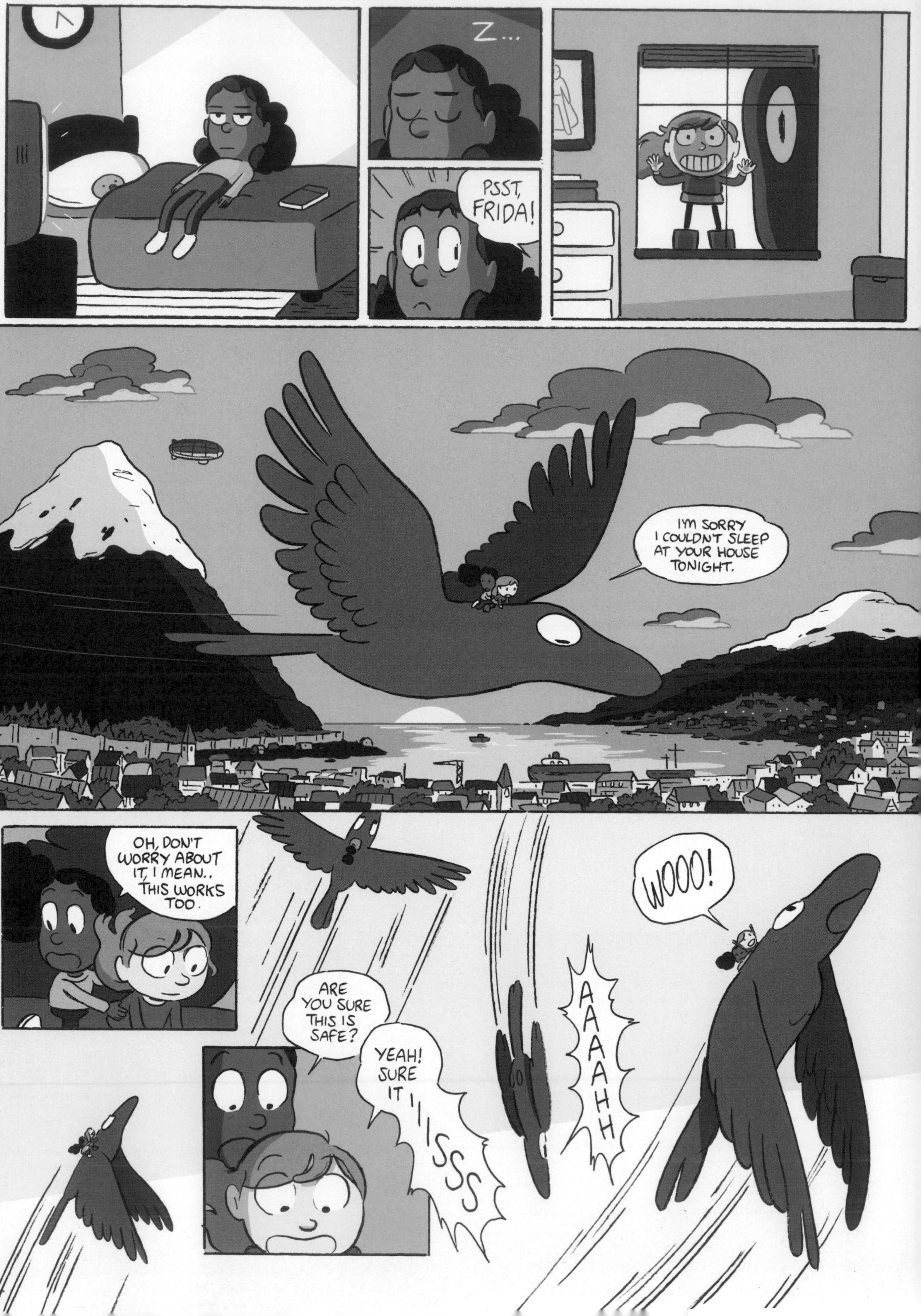
Z...
PSST, FRIDA!
I'M SORRY I COULDN'T SLEEP AT YOUR HOUSE TONIGHT.
OH, DON'T WORRY ABOUT IT, I MEAN.. THIS WORKS TOO.
ARE YOU SURE THIS IS SAFE?
YEAH! SURE IT IIISSSS
AAAAAHH
WOOO!

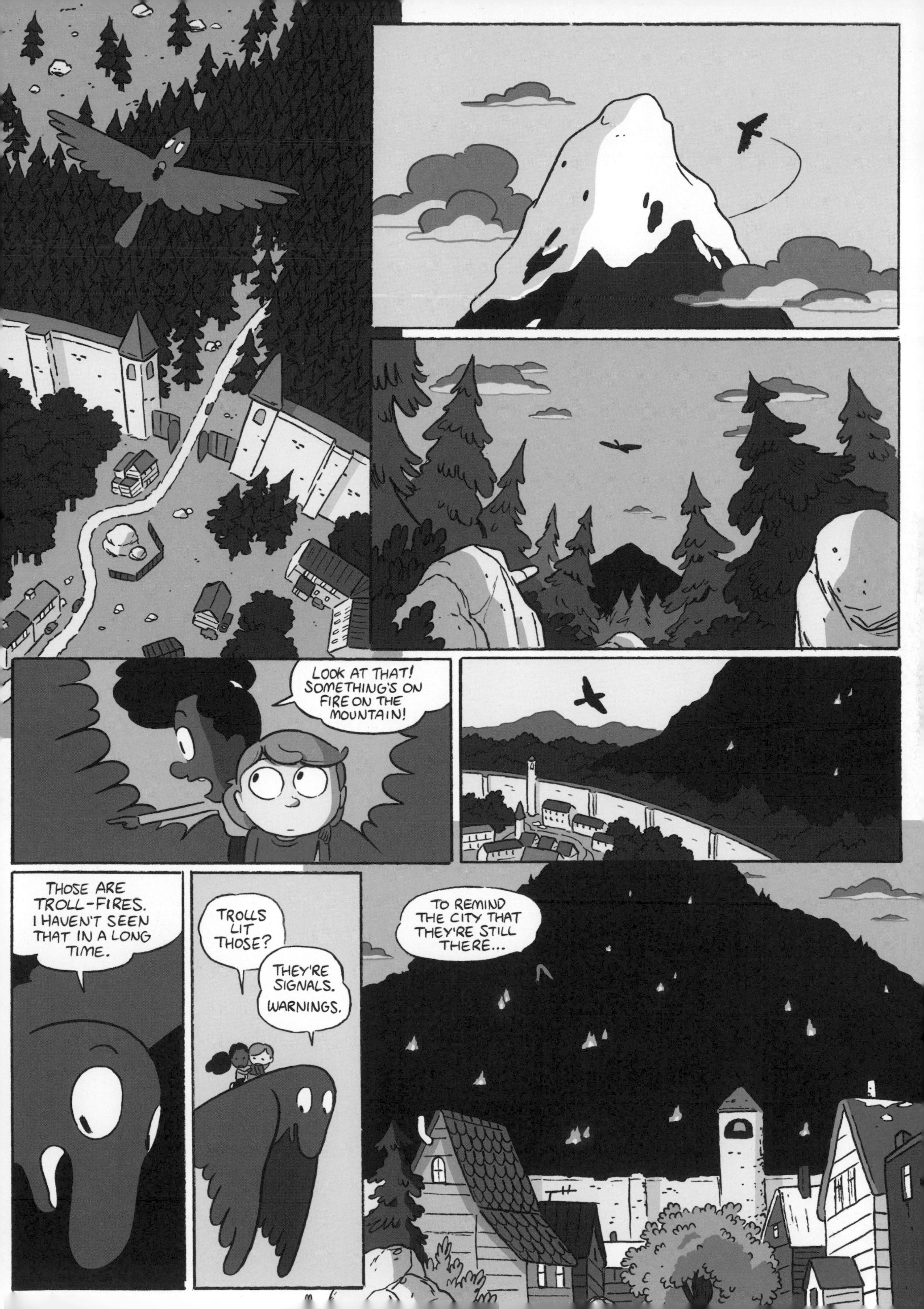
LOOK AT THAT! SOMETHING'S ON FIRE ON THE MOUNTAIN!
THOSE ARE TROLL-FIRES. I HAVEN'T SEEN THAT IN A LONG TIME.
TROLLS LIT THOSE?
THEY'RE SIGNALS. WARNINGS.
TO REMIND THE CITY THAT THEY'RE STILL THERE...

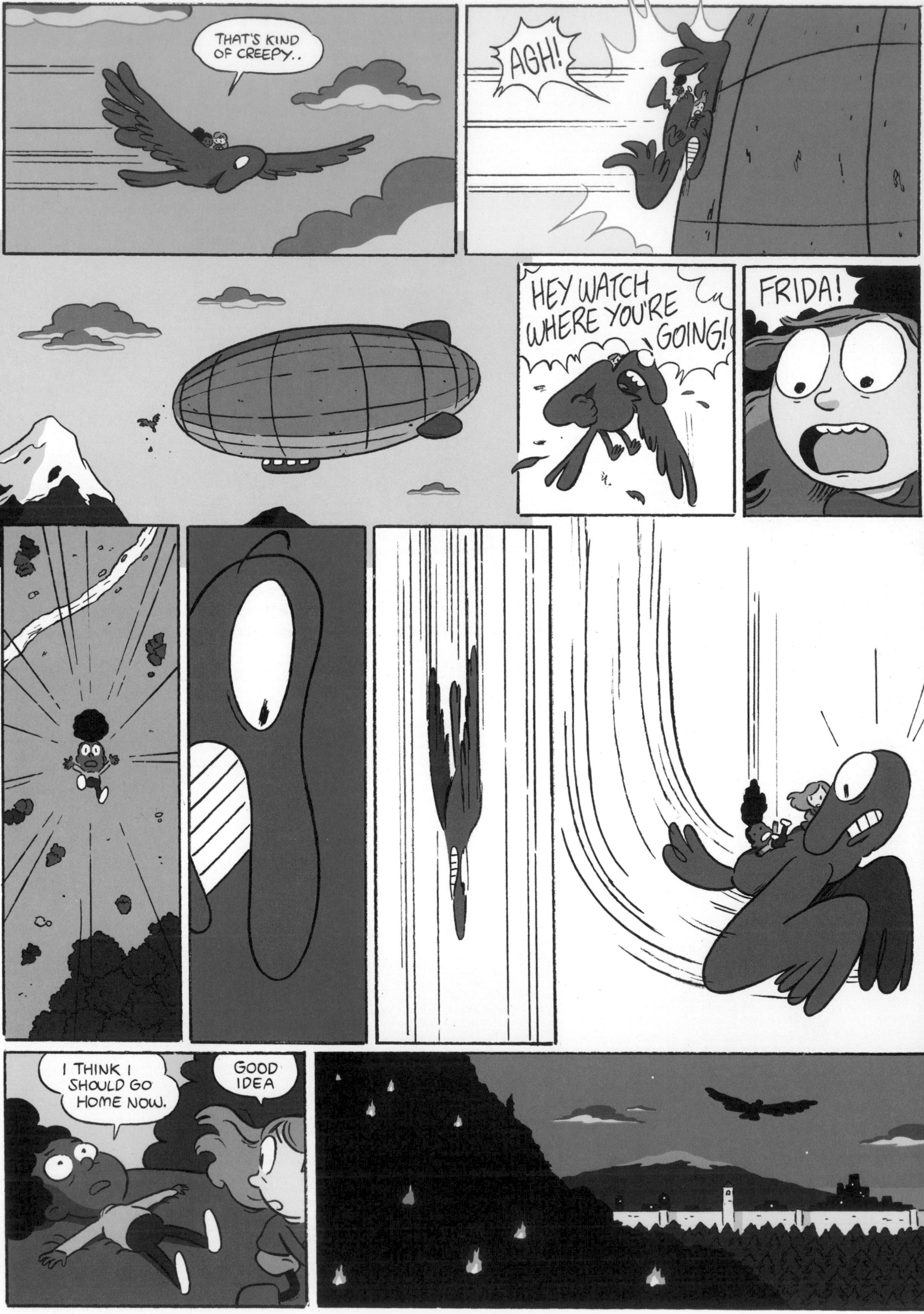
THAT'S KIND OF CREEPY..
AGH!
HEY WATCH WHERE YOU'RE GOING!
FRIDA!
I THINK I SHOULD GO HOME NOW.
GOOD IDEA

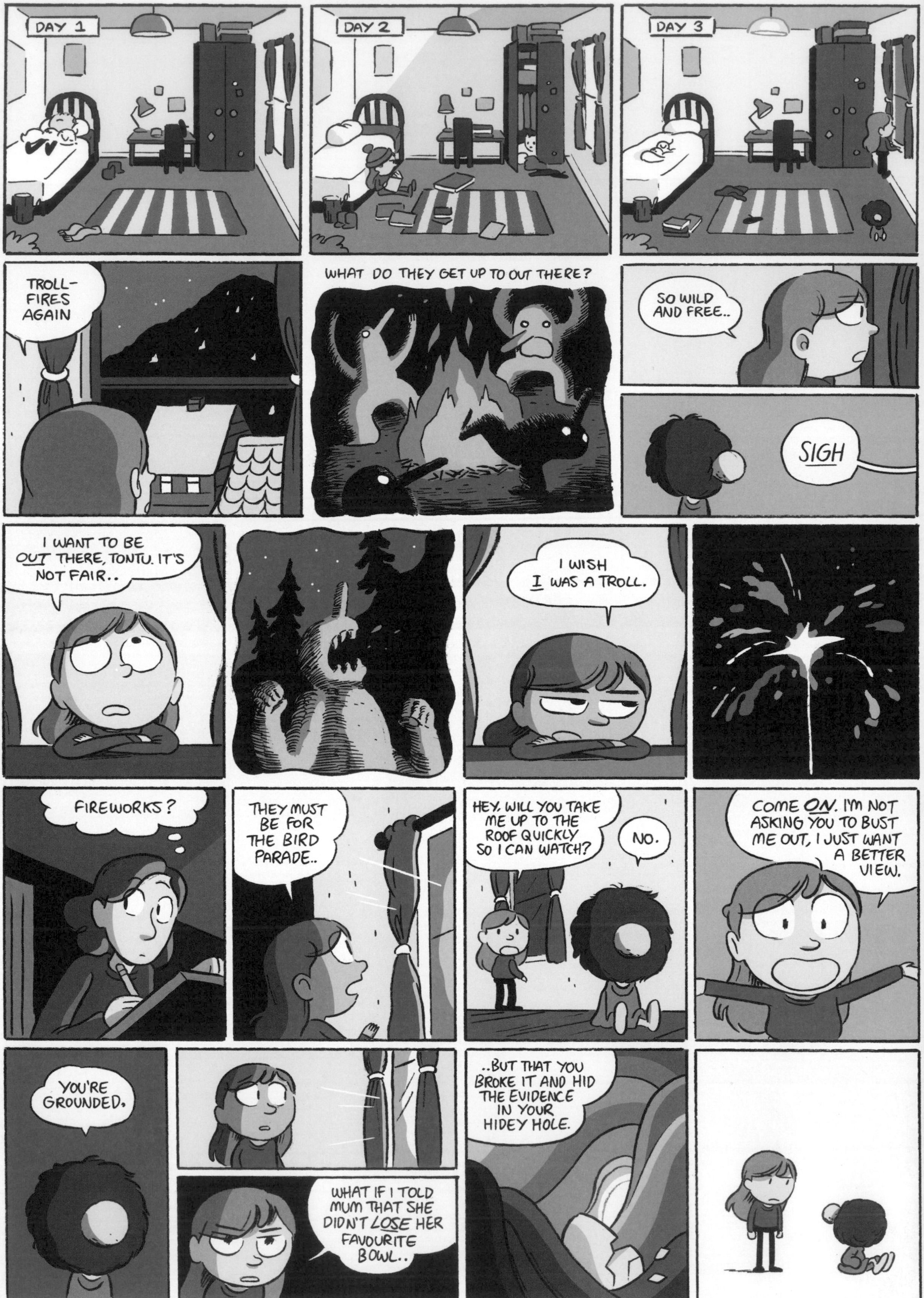
DAY 1
DAY 2
DAY 3
TROLL-FIRES AGAIN
WHAT DO THEY GET UP TO OUT THERE?
SO WILD AND FREE..
SIGH
I WANT TO BE OUT THERE, TONTU. IT'S NOT FAIR..
I WISH I WAS A TROLL.
FIREWORKS?
THEY MUST BE FOR THE BIRD PARADE..
HEY, WILL YOU TAKE ME UP TO THE ROOF QUICKLY SO I CAN WATCH?
NO.
COME ON. I'M NOT ASKING YOU TO BUST ME OUT, I JUST WANT A BETTER VIEW.
YOU'RE GROUNDED.
WHAT IF I TOLD MUM THAT SHE DIDN'T LOSE HER FAVOURITE BOWL..
..BUT THAT YOU BROKE IT AND HID THE EVIDENCE IN YOUR HIDEY HOLE.

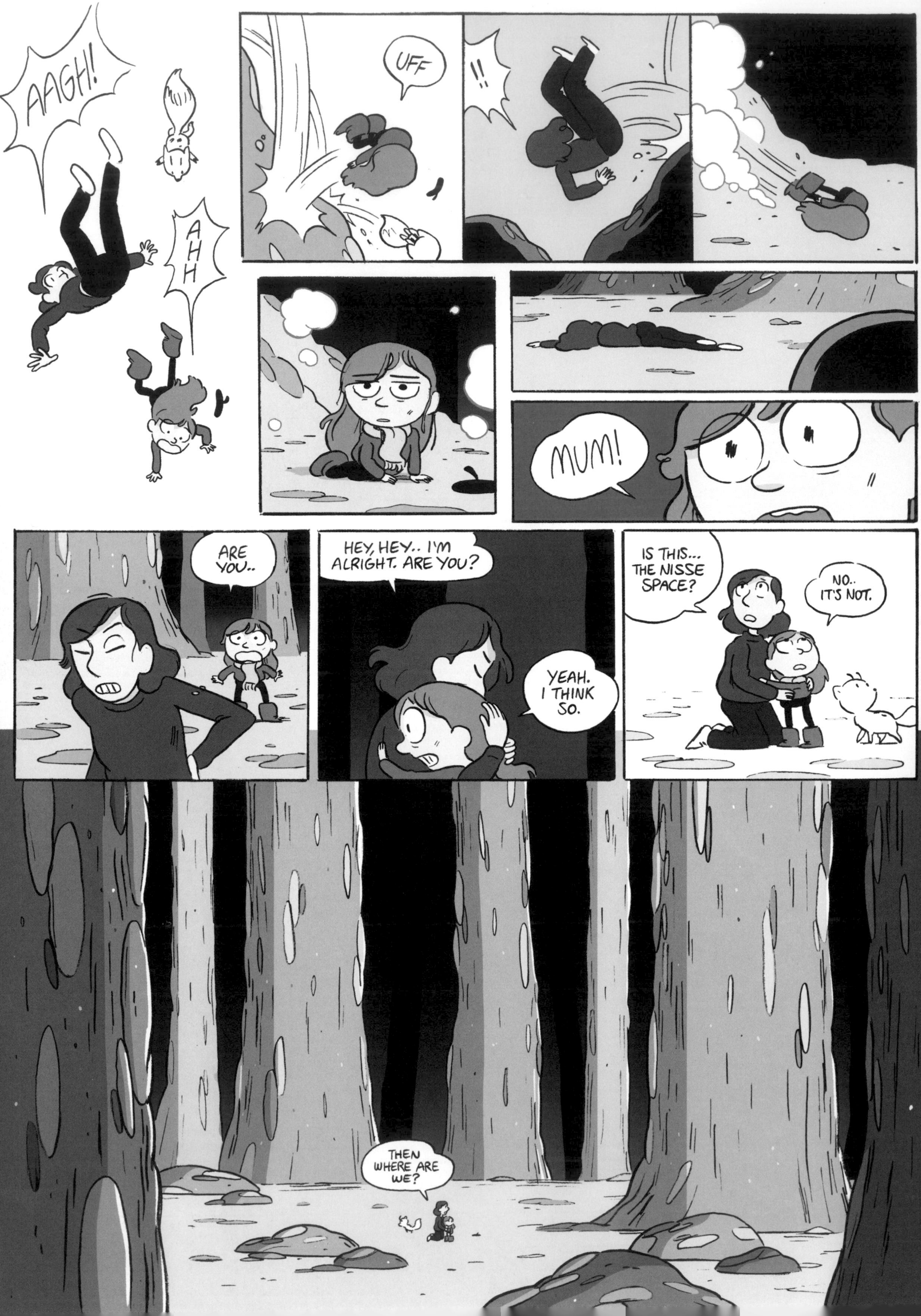
AAGH!
AHH
UFF
!!
MUM!
ARE YOU..
HEY, HEY.. I'M ALRIGHT. ARE YOU?
YEAH. I THINK SO.
IS THIS... THE NISSE SPACE?
NO.. IT'S NOT.
THEN WHERE ARE WE?

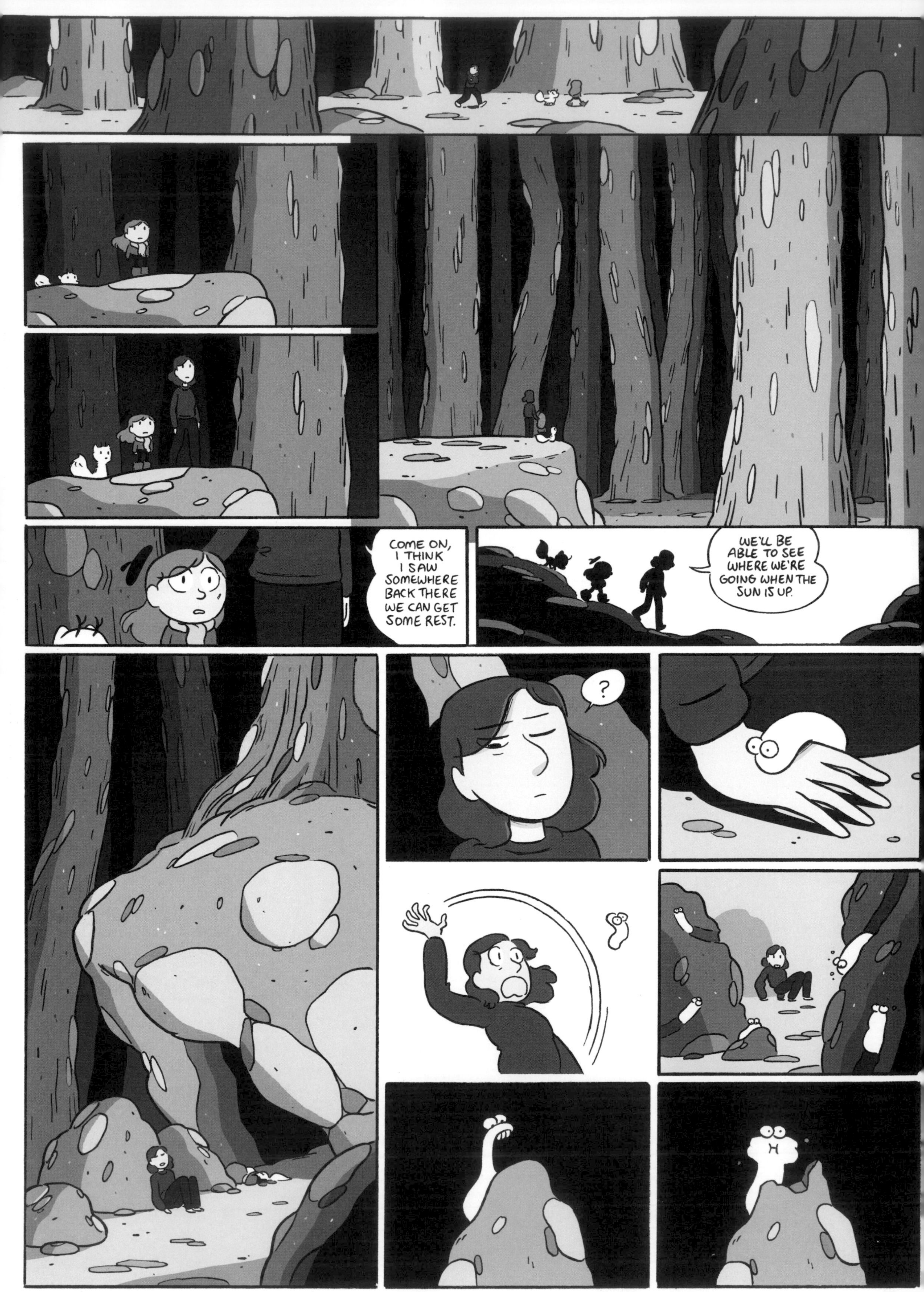
COME ON, I THINK I SAW SOMEWHERE BACK THERE WE CAN GET SOME REST.
WE'LL BE ABLE TO SEE WHERE WE'RE GOING WHEN THE SUN IS UP.
?

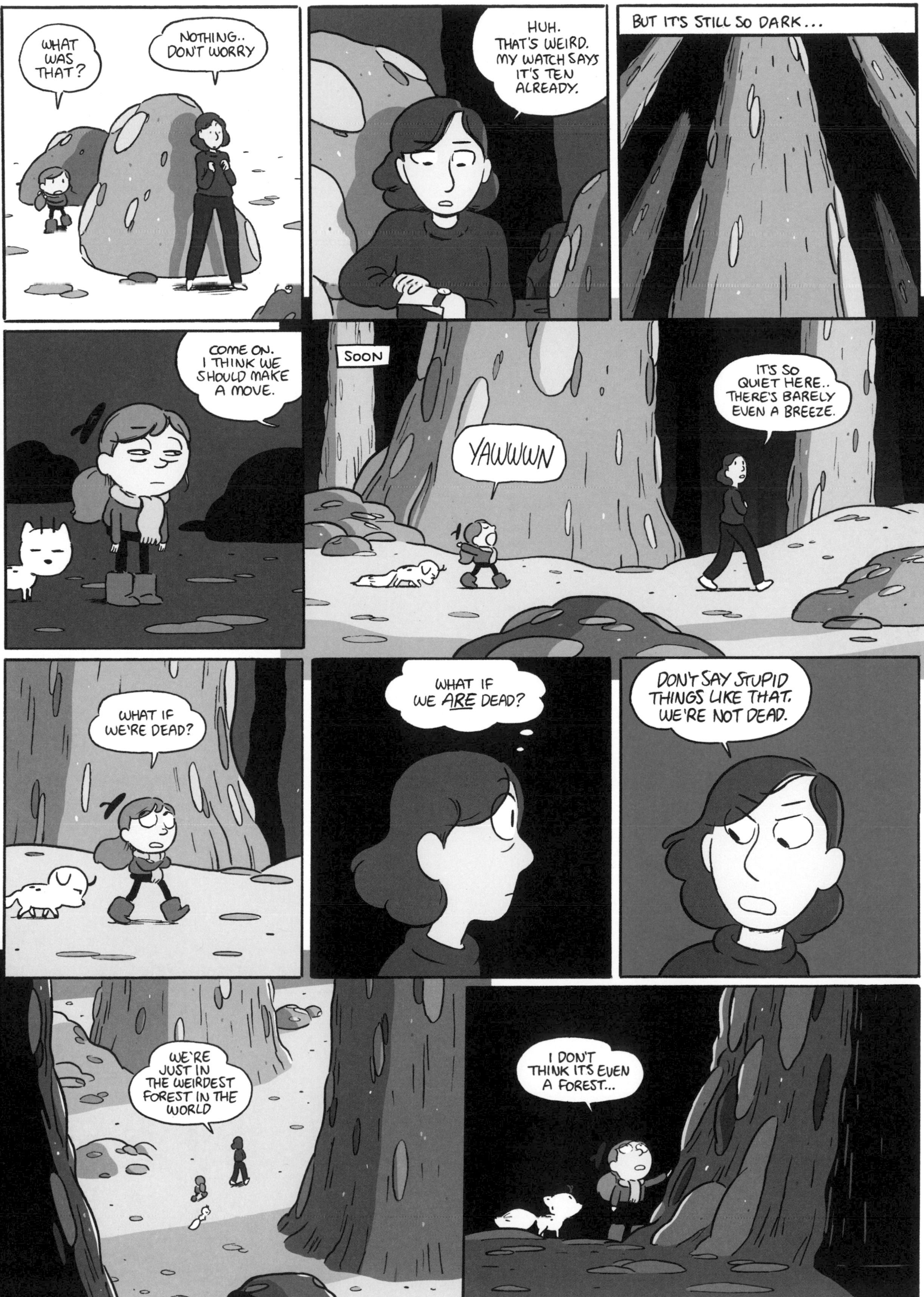
WHAT WAS THAT?
NOTHING.. DON'T WORRY
HUH. THAT'S WEIRD. MY WATCH SAYS IT'S TEN ALREADY.
BUT IT'S STILL SO DARK...
COME ON. I THINK WE SHOULD MAKE A MOVE.
SOON
YAWWWN
IT'S SO QUIET HERE.. THERE'S BARELY EVEN A BREEZE.
WHAT IF WE'RE DEAD?
WHAT IF WE ARE DEAD?
DON'T SAY STUPID THINGS LIKE THAT. WE'RE NOT DEAD.
WE'RE JUST IN THE WEIRDEST FOREST IN THE WORLD
I DON'T THINK IT'S EVEN A FOREST...

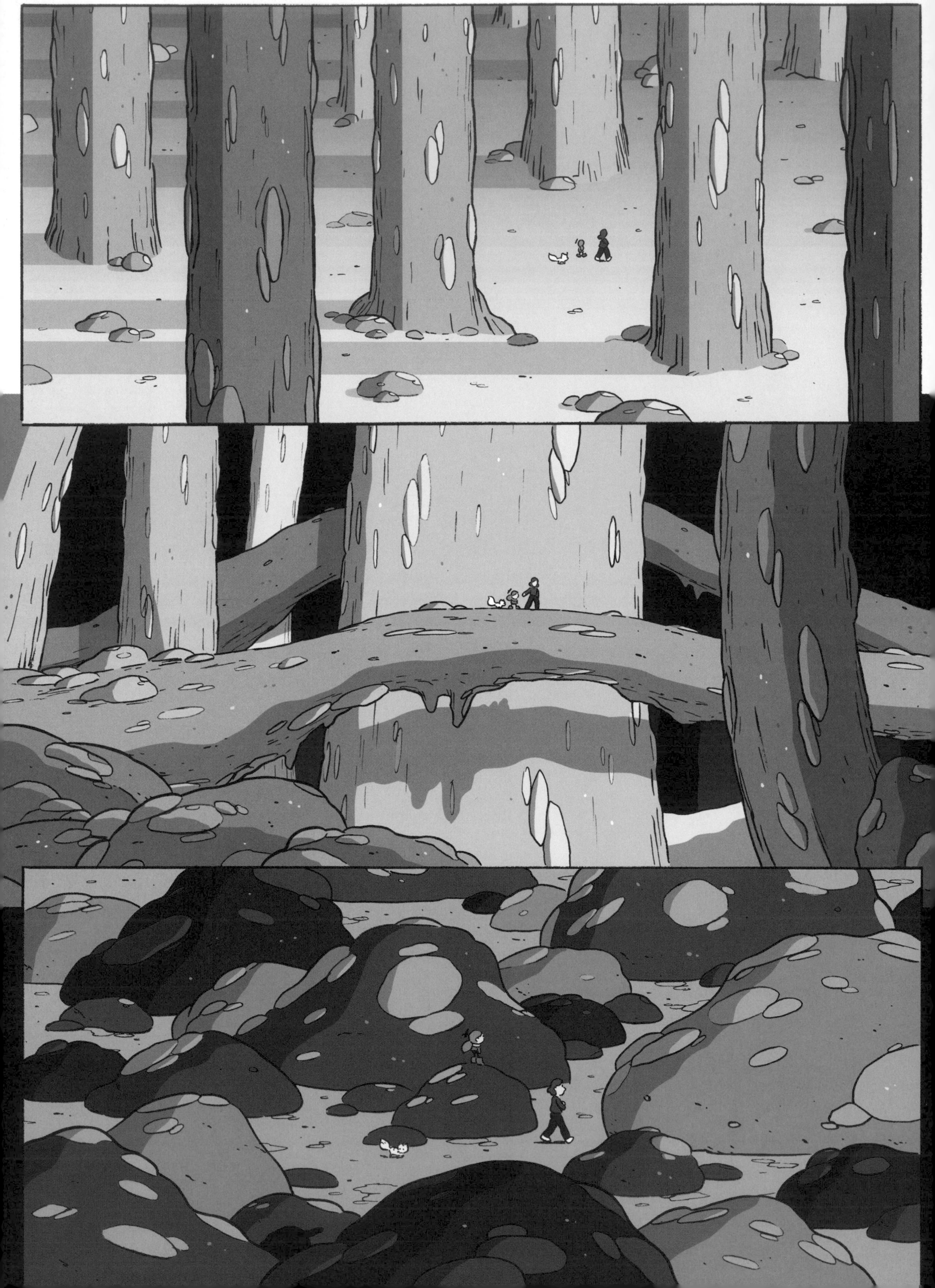

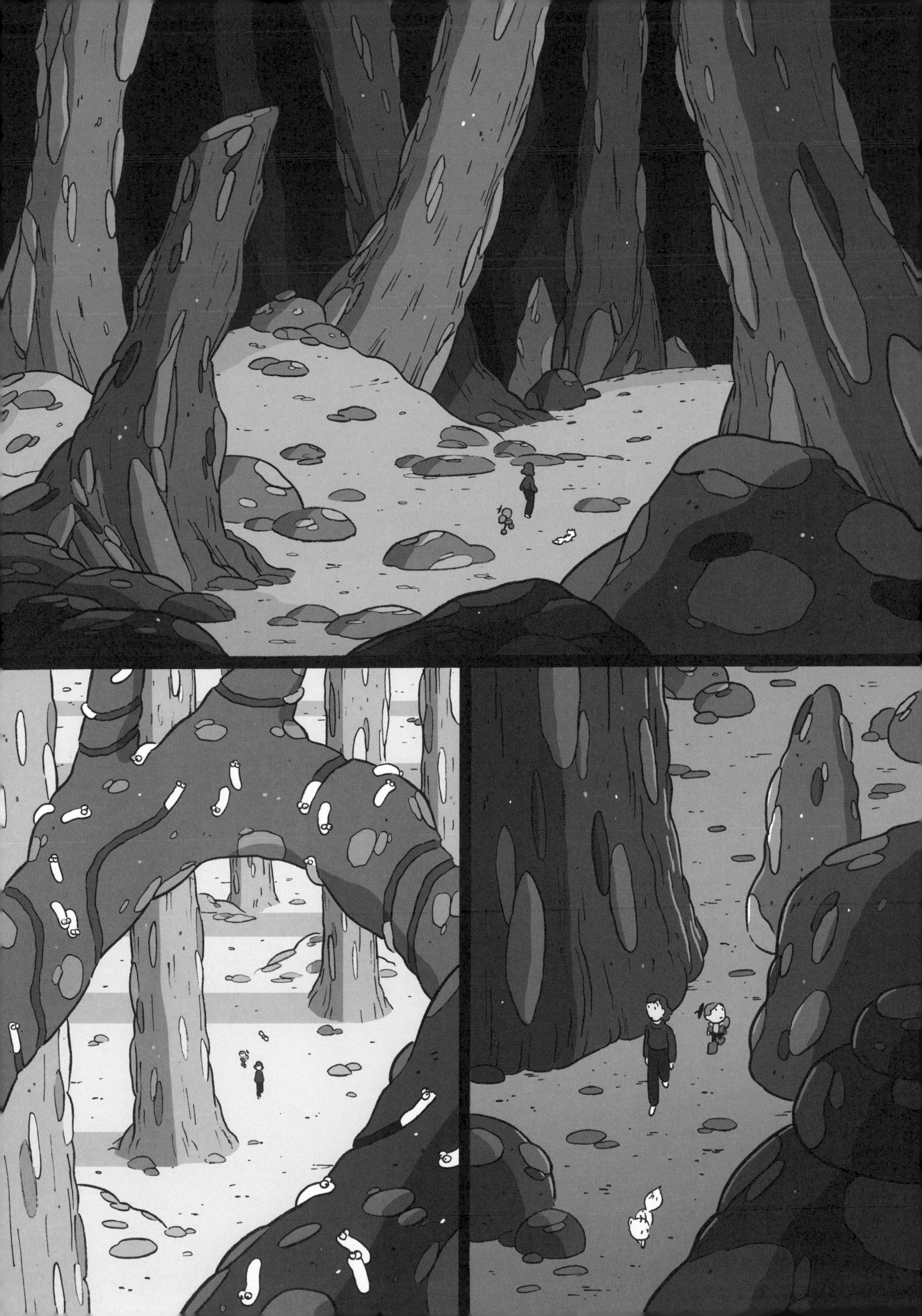

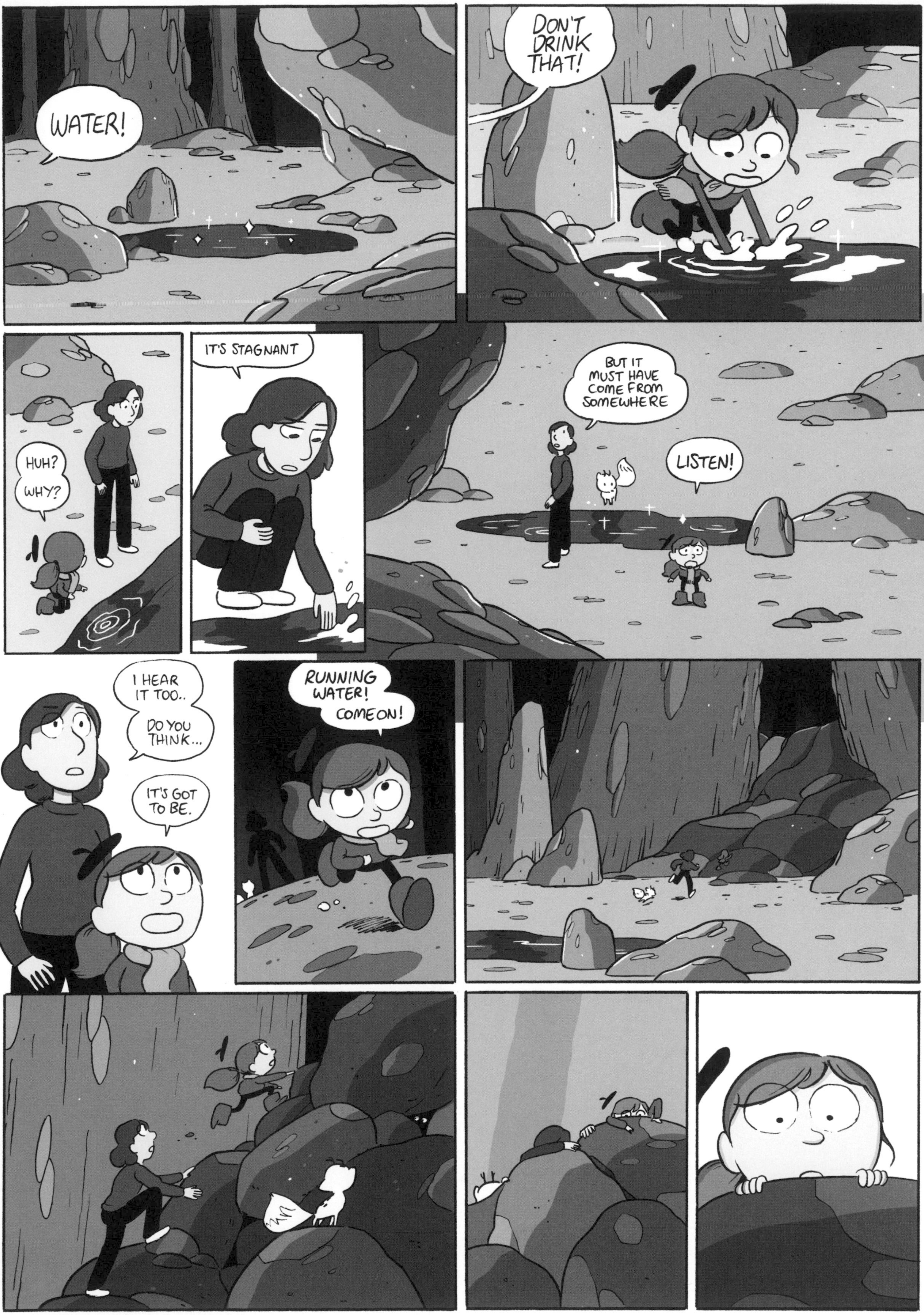
WATER!
DON'T DRINK THAT!
HUH?
WHY?
IT'S STAGNANT
BUT IT MUST HAVE COME FROM SOMEWHERE
LISTEN!
I HEAR IT TOO..
DO YOU THINK...
IT'S GOT TO BE.
RUNNING WATER!
COME ON!

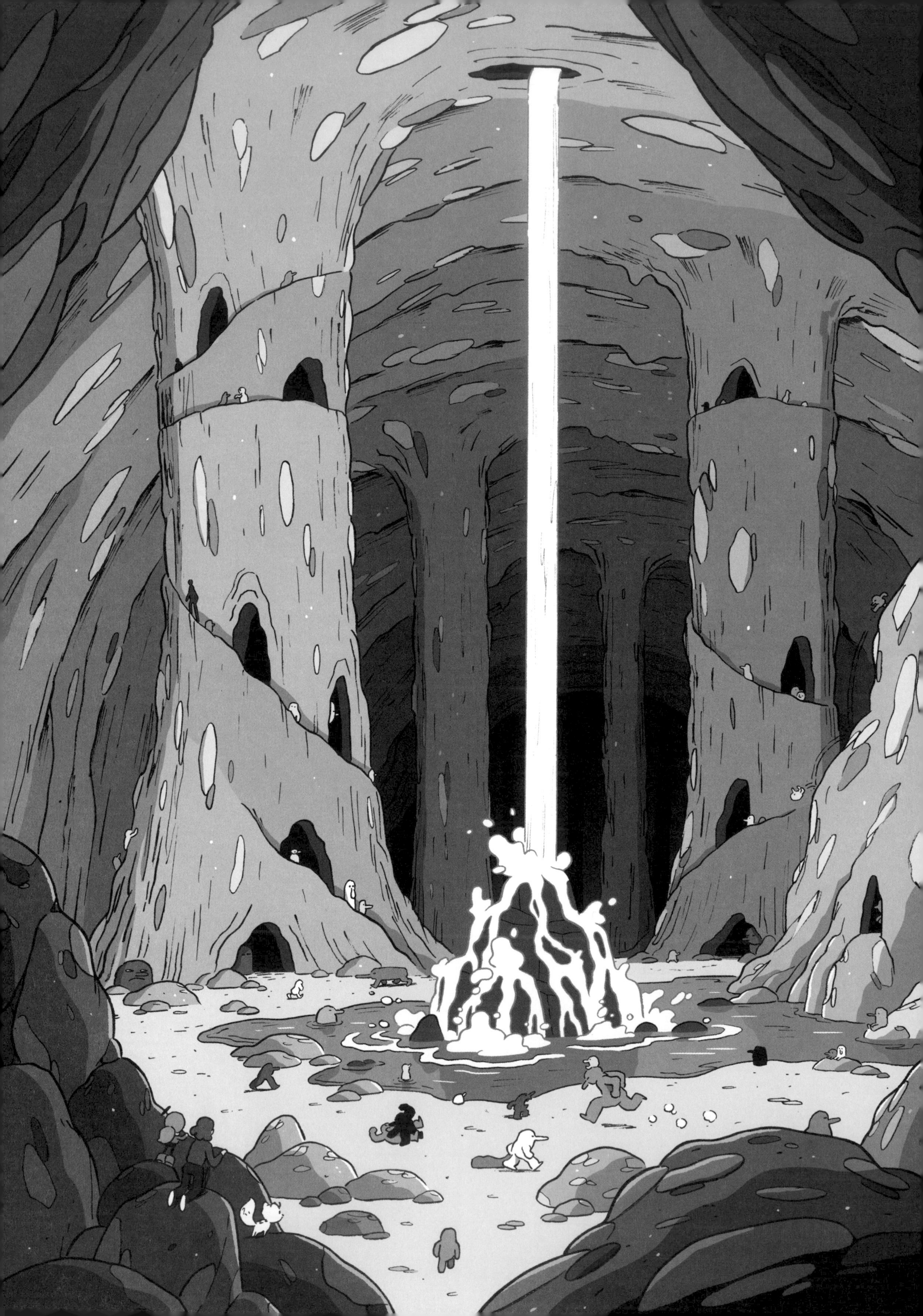

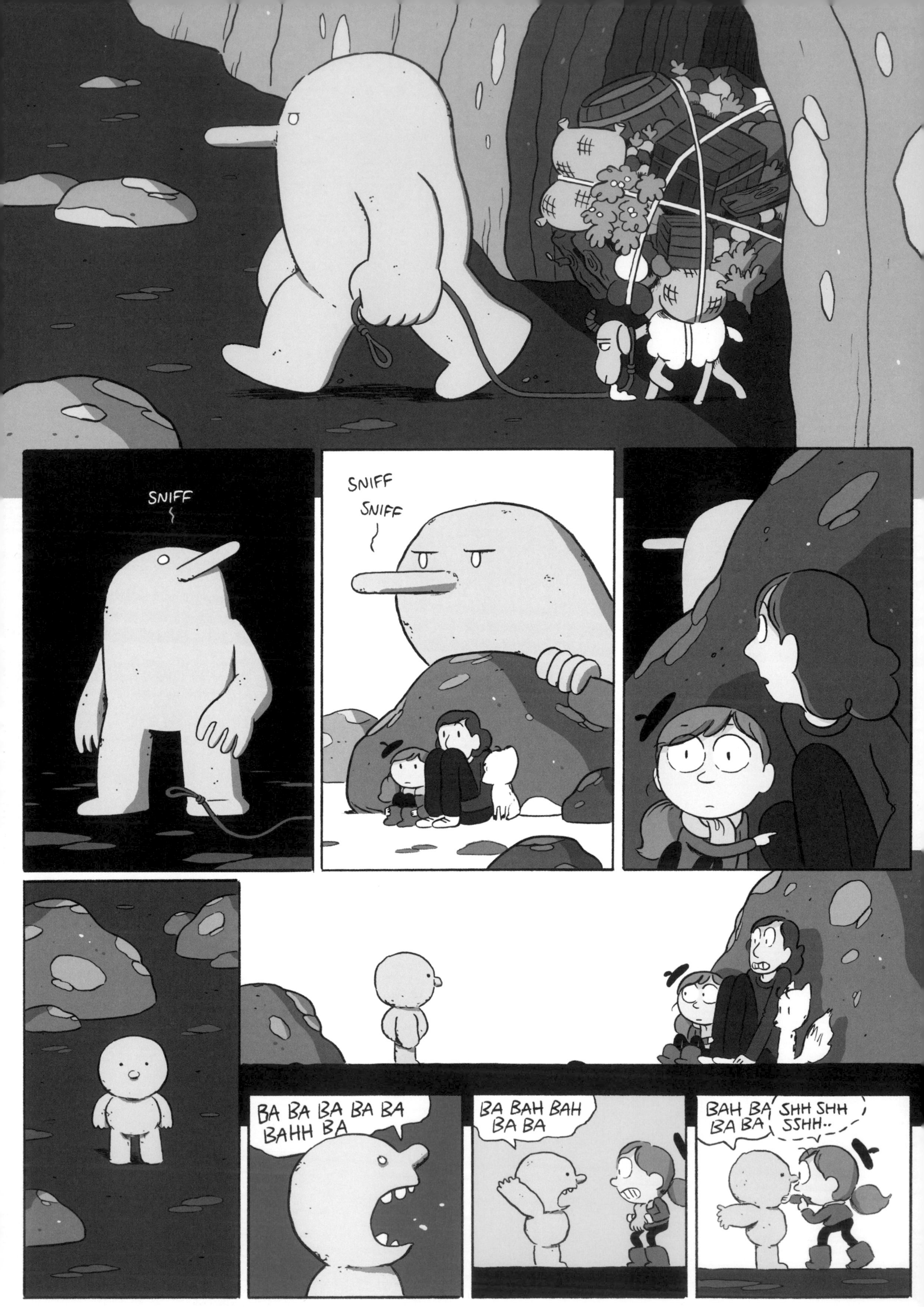

SNIFF
SNIFF
SNIFF
BA BA BA BA BA BAHH BA
BA BAH BAH BA BA
BAH BA BA BA
SHH SHH SSHH..

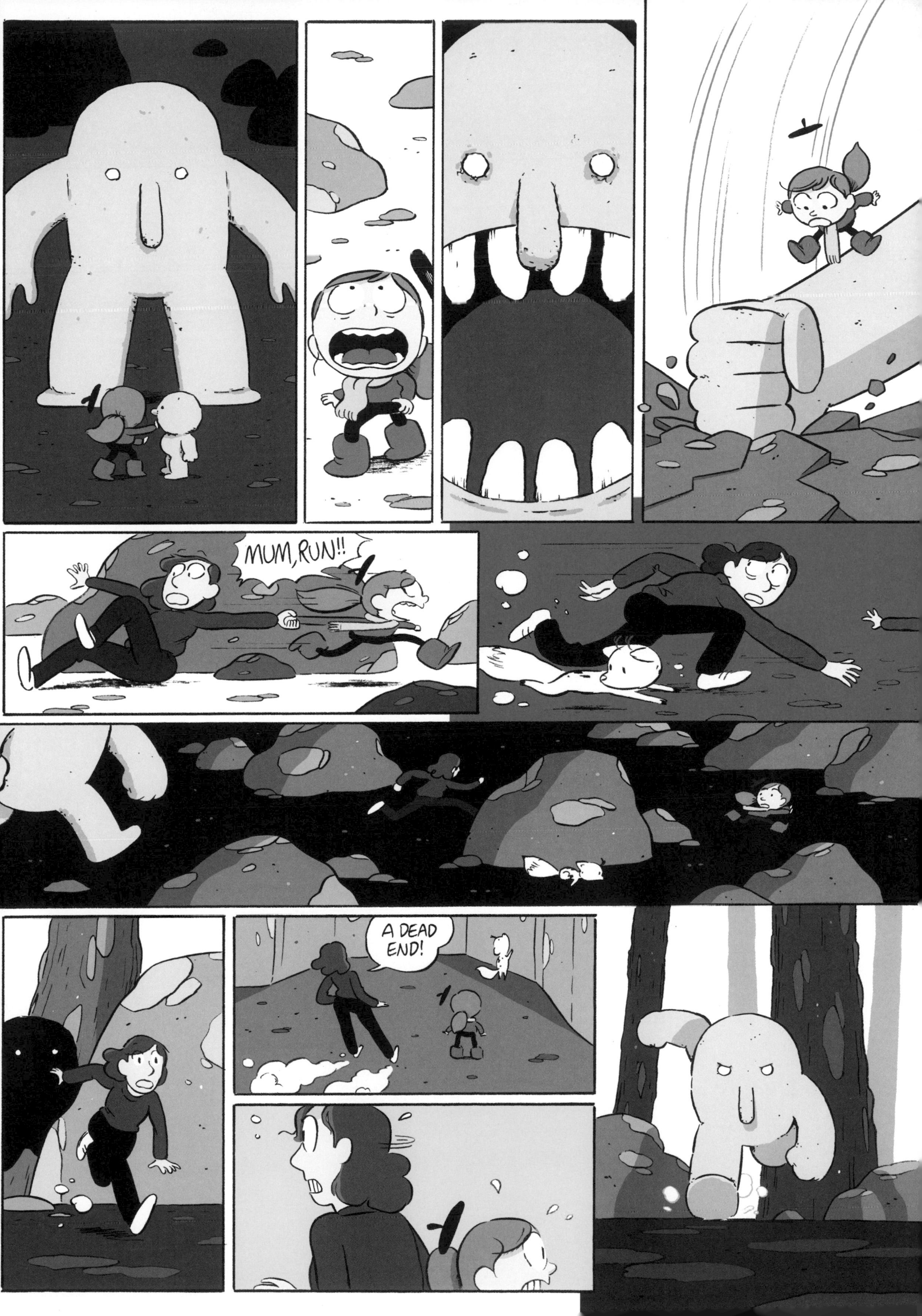
MUM, RUN!!
A DEAD END!

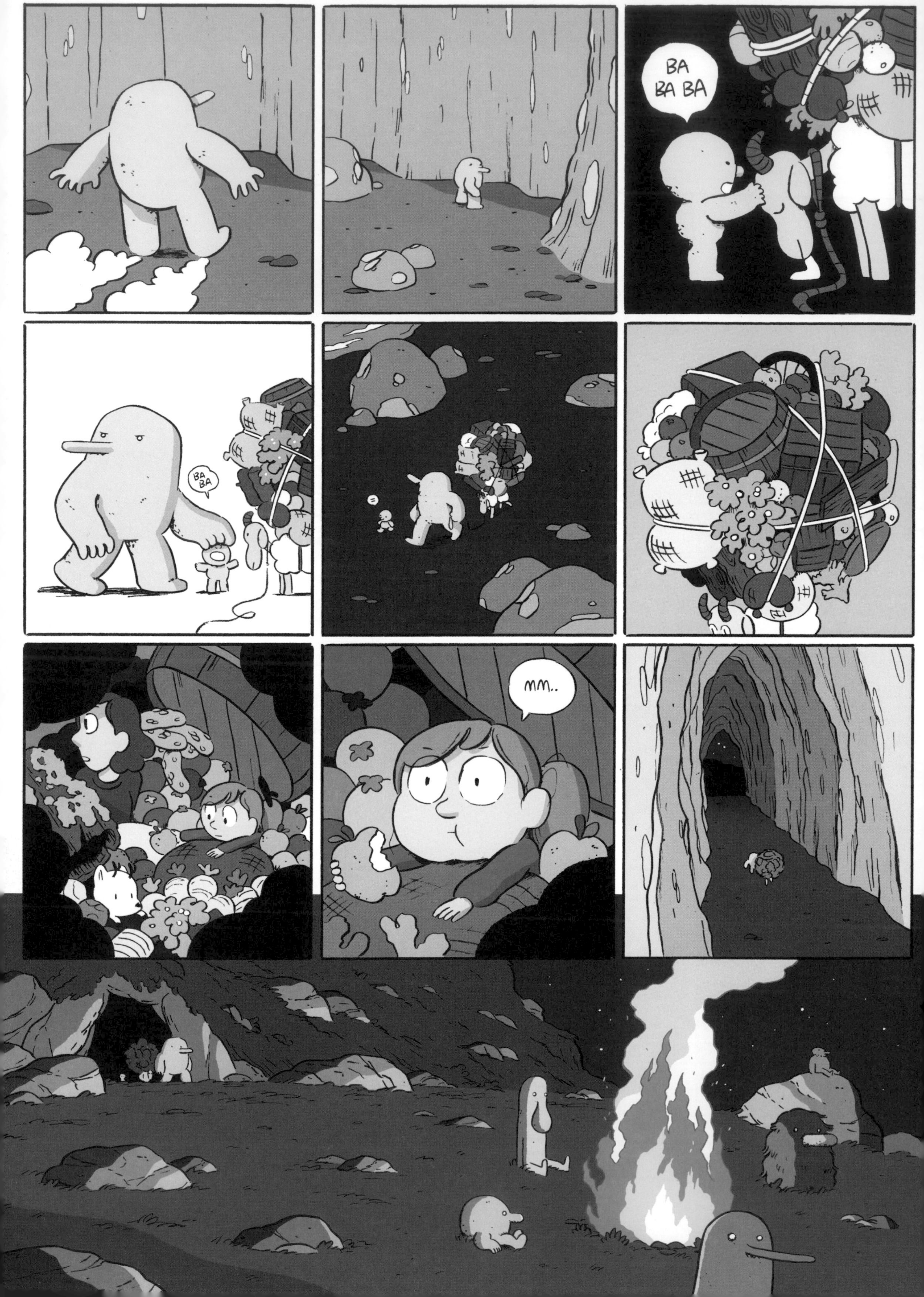
BA
BA BA
BA
BA
MM..

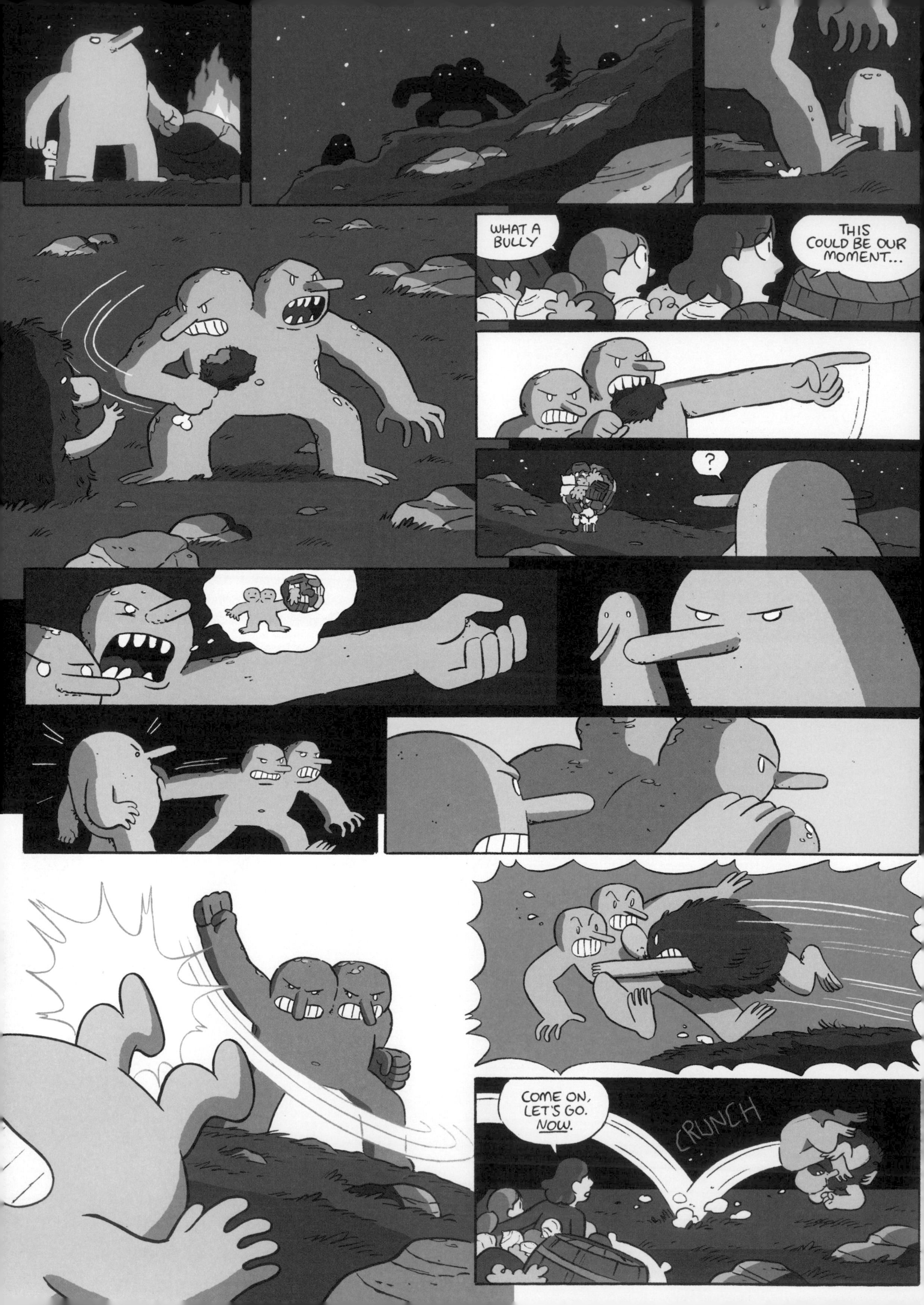
WHAT A BULLY
THIS COULD BE OUR MOMENT...
?
COME ON, LET'S GO. NOW.
CRUNCH

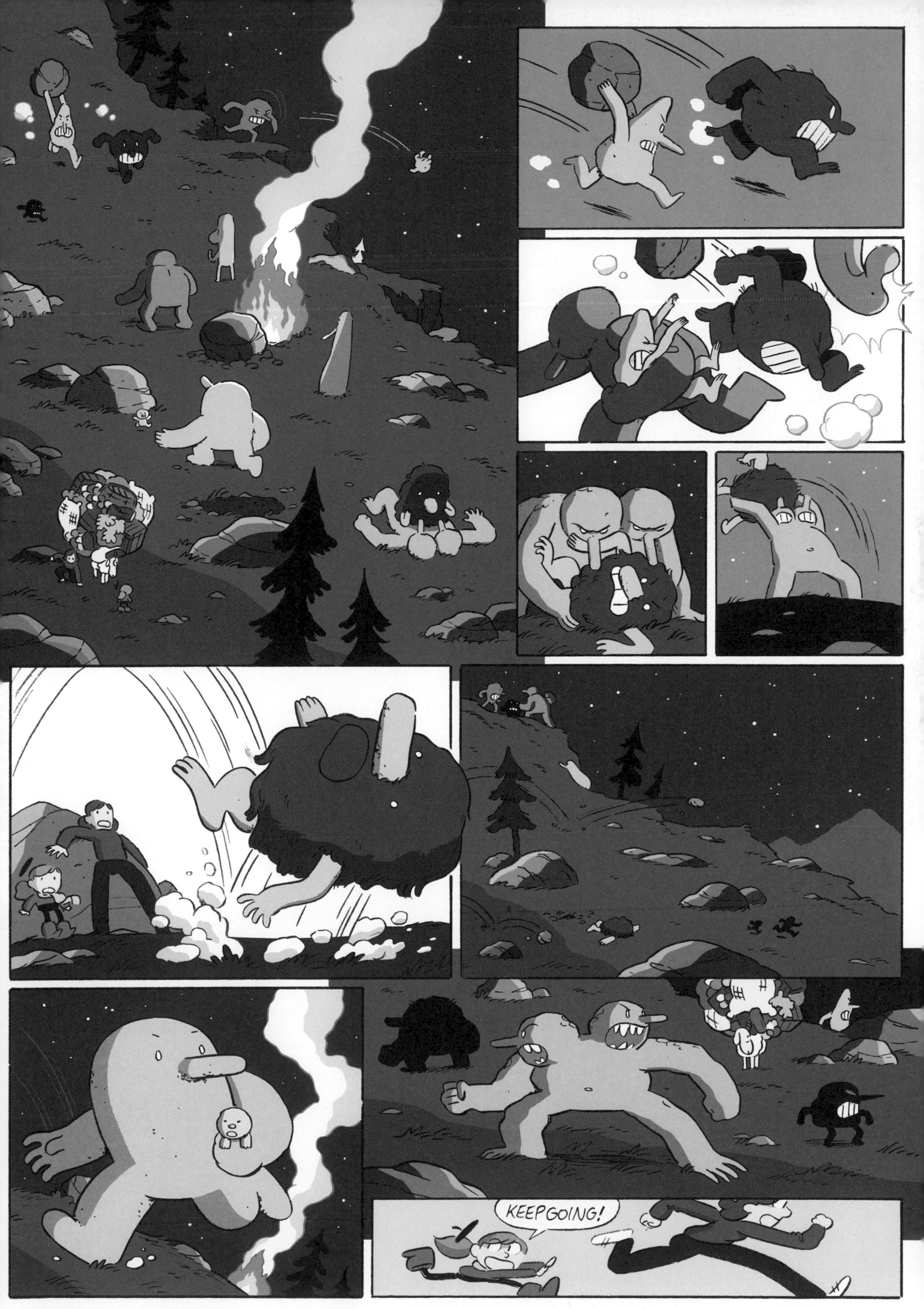
KEEPGOING!

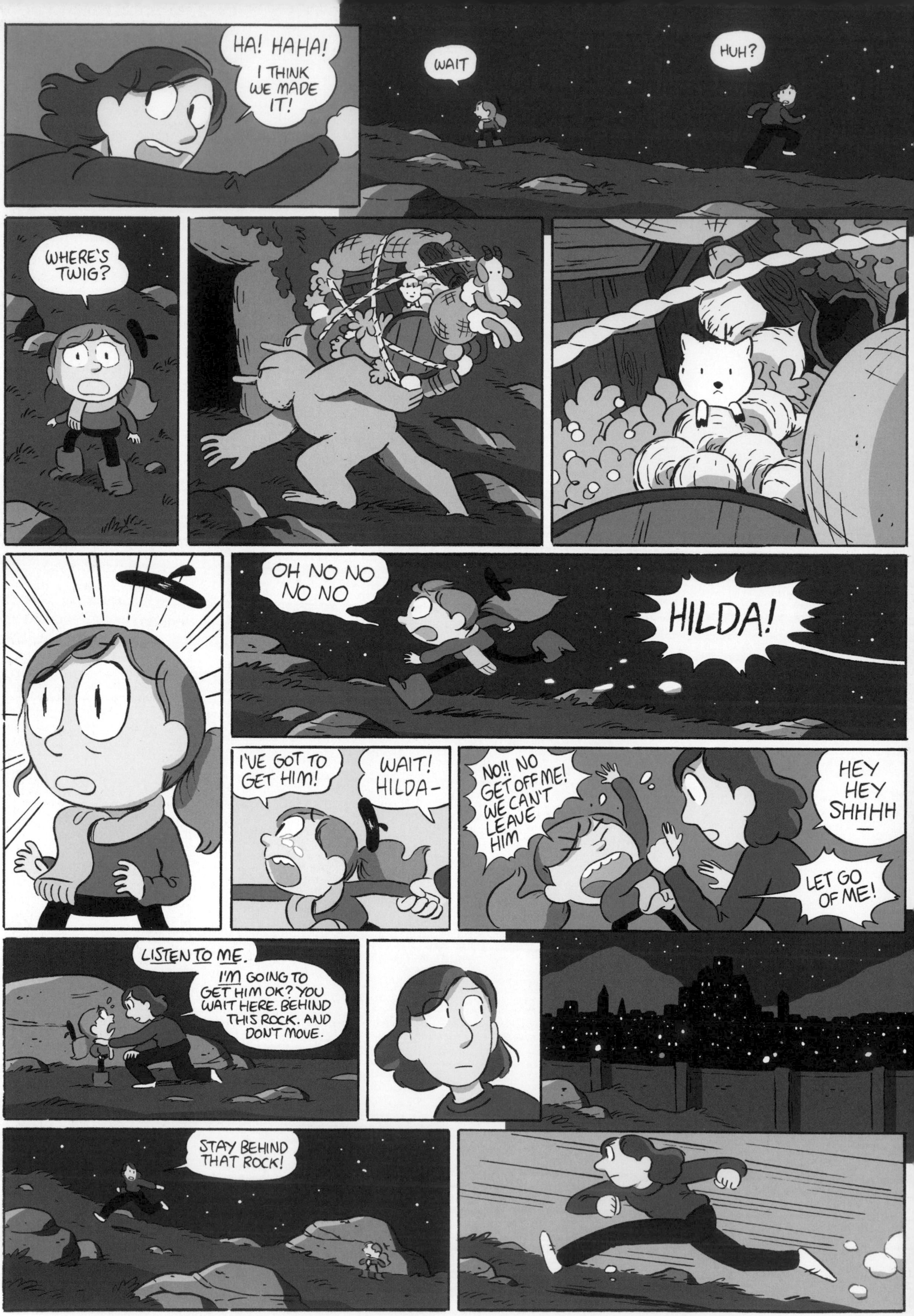
HA! HAHA!
I THINK WE MADE IT!
WAIT
HUH?
WHERE'S TWIG?
OH NO NO NO NO
HILDA!
I'VE GOT TO GET HIM!
WAIT! HILDA-
NO!! NO GET OFF ME! WE CAN'T LEAVE HIM
HEY HEY SHHHH —
LET GO OF ME!
LISTEN TO ME.
I'M GOING TO GET HIM OK? YOU WAIT HERE. BEHIND THIS ROCK. AND DON'T MOVE.
STAY BEHIND THAT ROCK!

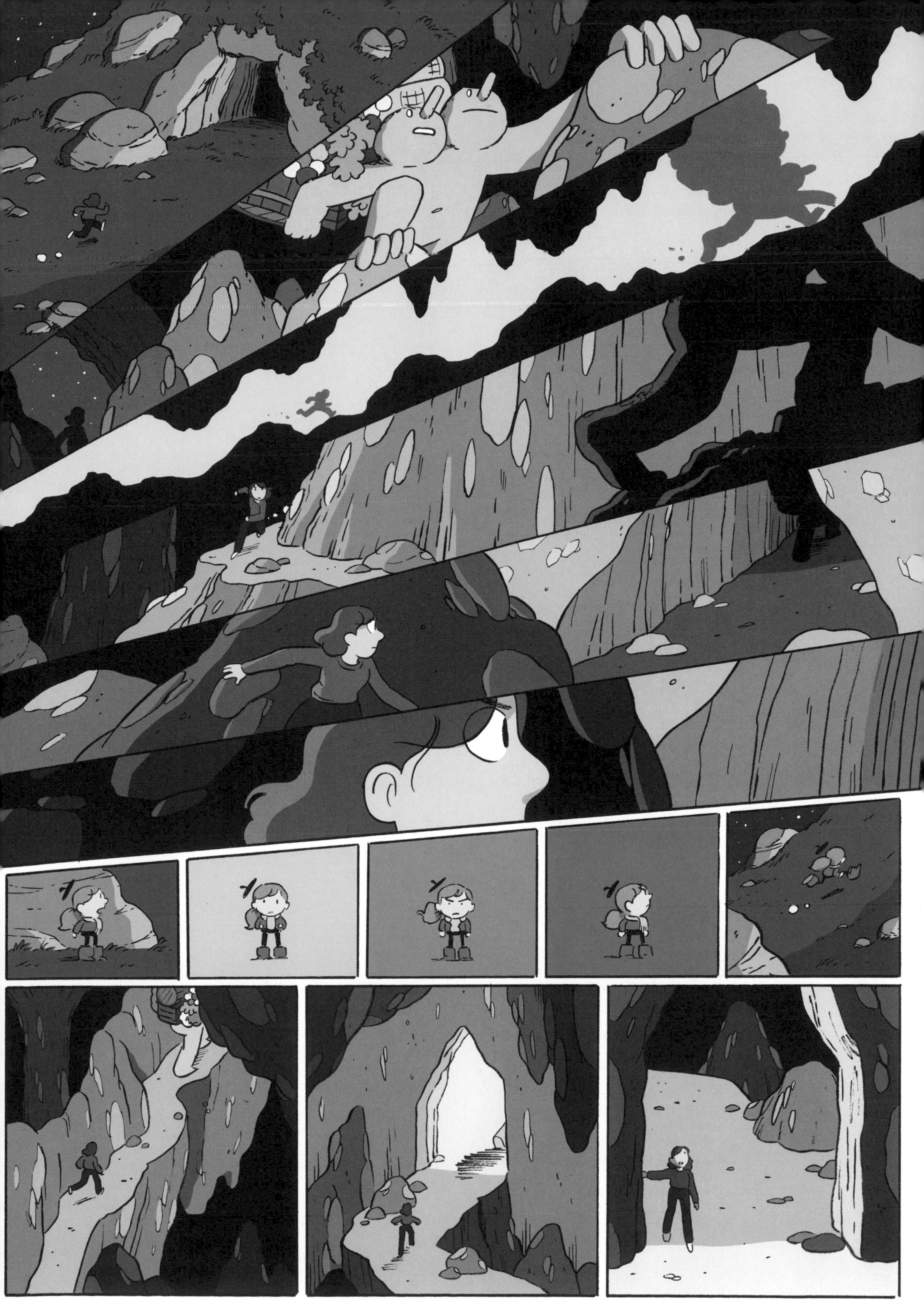

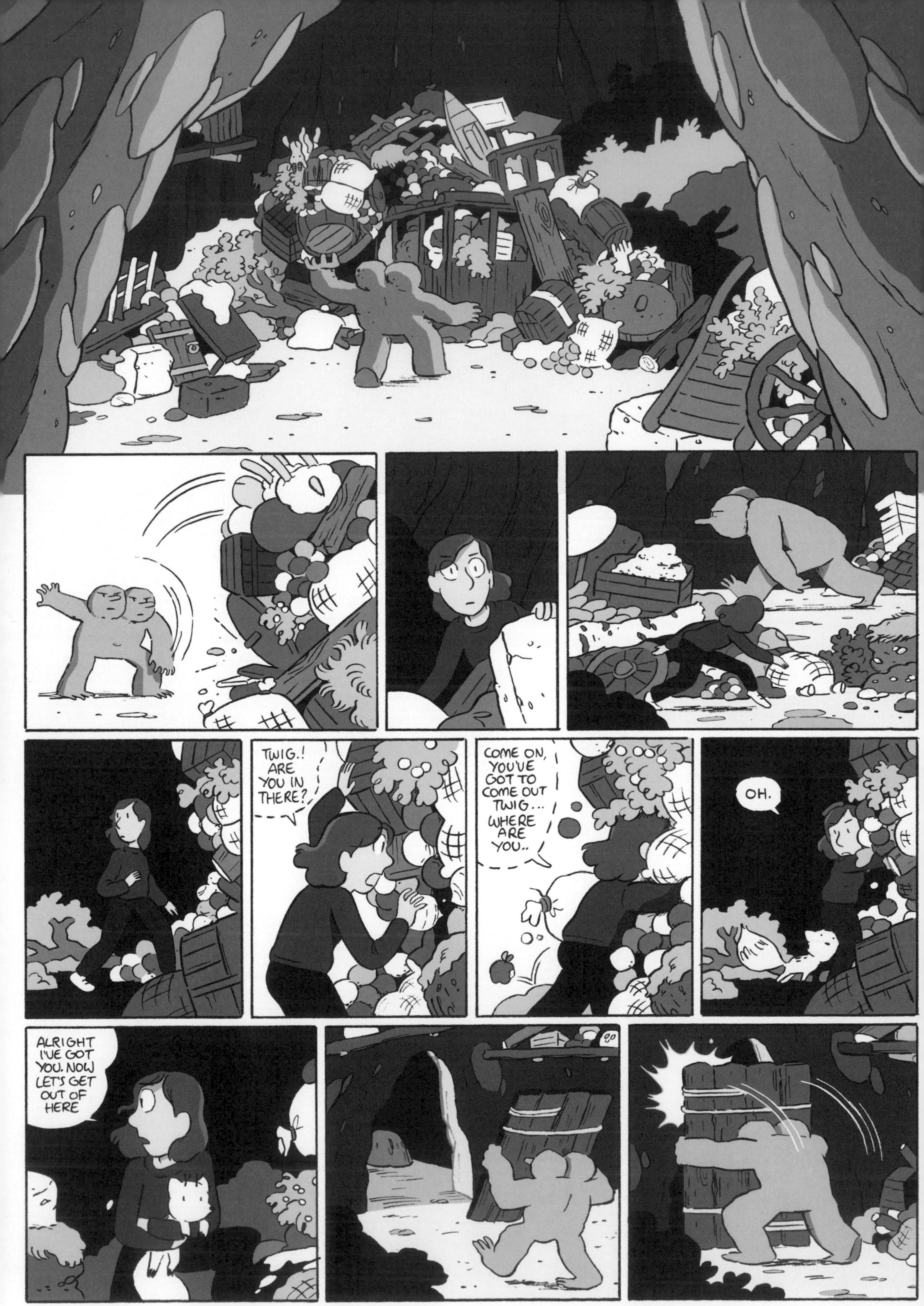
TWIG.! ARE YOU IN THERE?
COME ON, YOU'VE GOT TO COME OUT TWIG... WHERE ARE YOU..
OH.
ALRIGHT I'VE GOT YOU. NOW LET'S GET OUT OF HERE

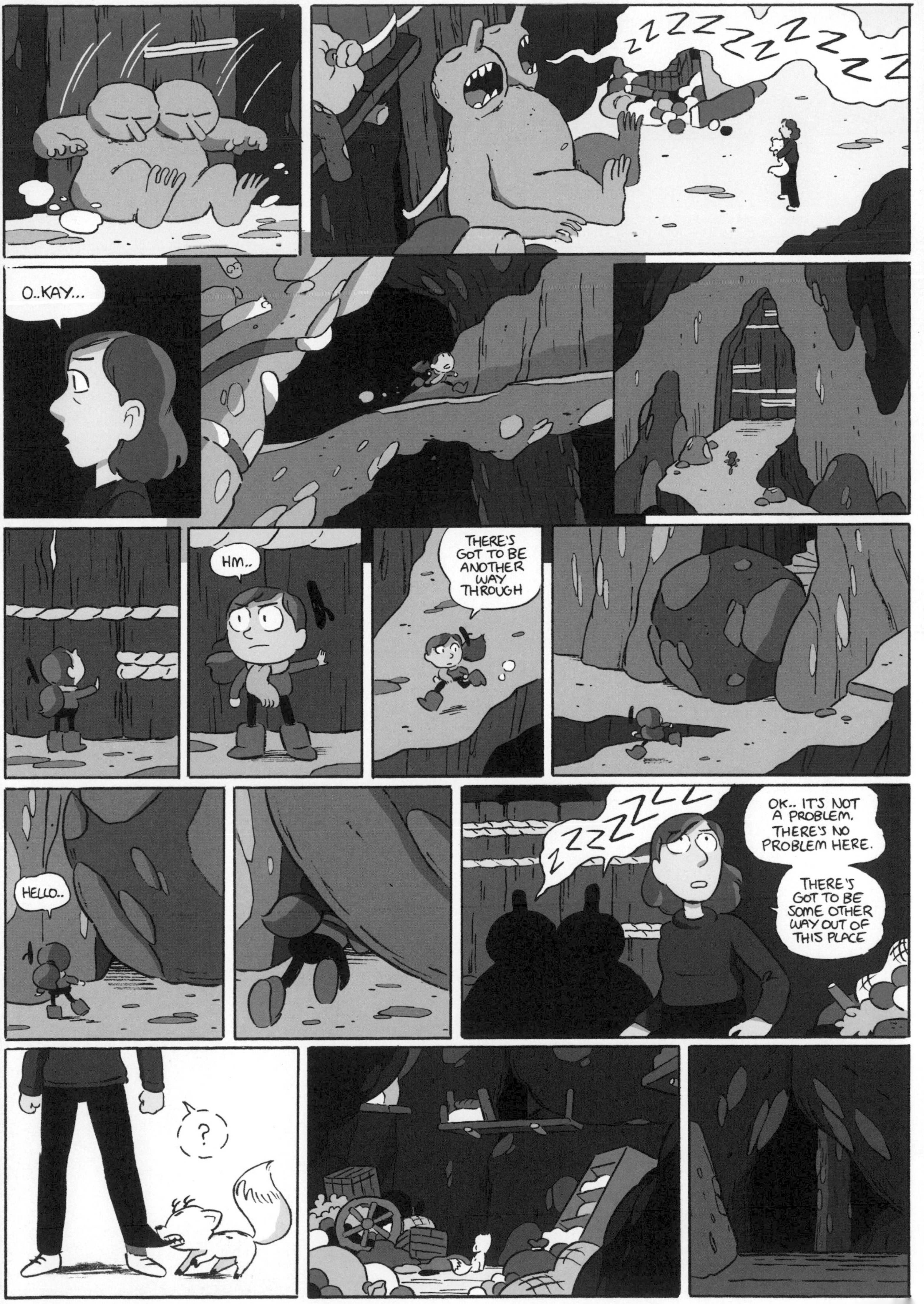
ZZZZZZZZZZZ
O..KAY...
HM..
THERE'S GOT TO BE ANOTHER WAY THROUGH
HELLO..
ZZZZZZZ
OK.. IT'S NOT A PROBLEM. THERE'S NO PROBLEM HERE.
THERE'S GOT TO BE SOME OTHER WAY OUT OF THIS PLACE
?

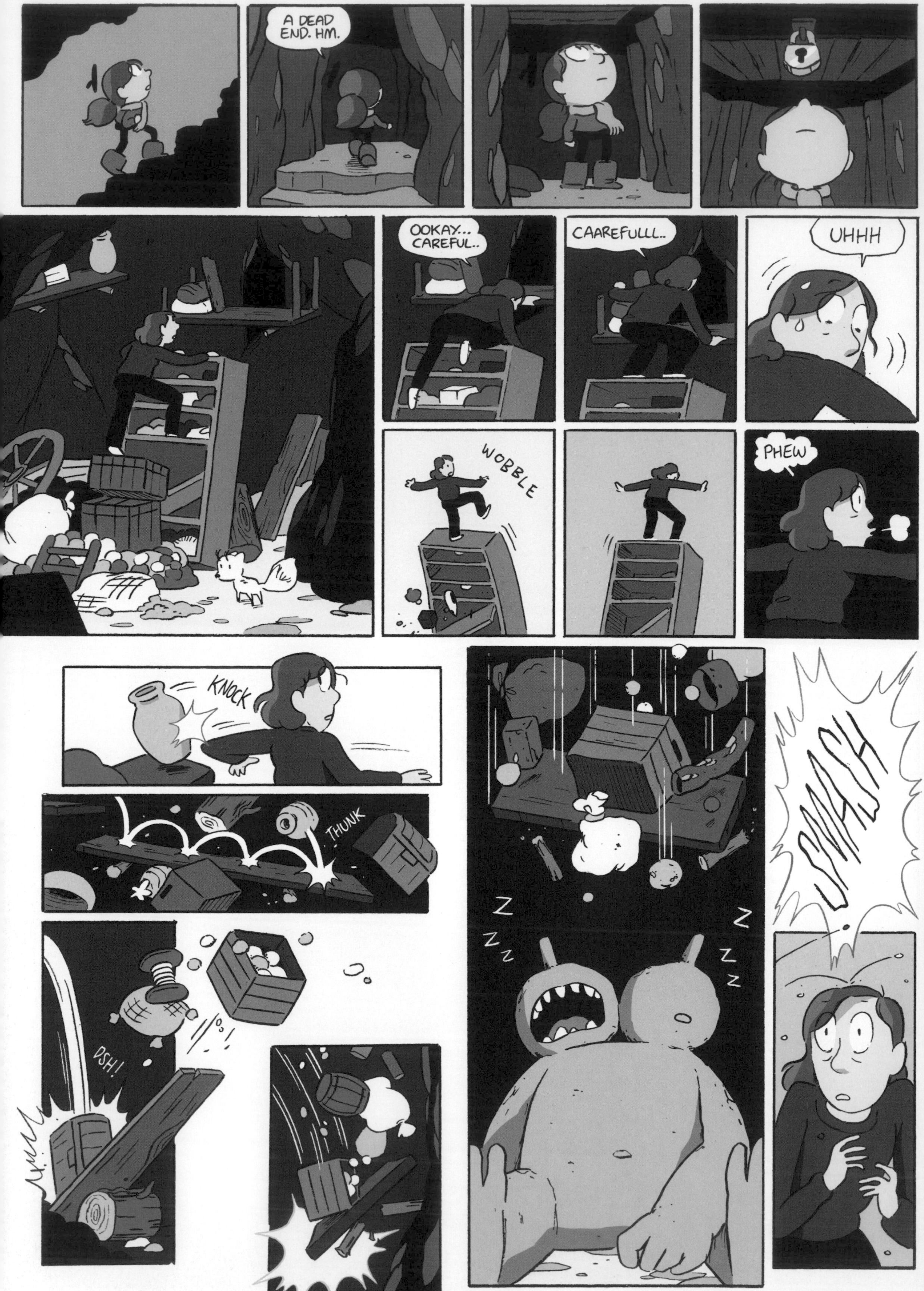
A DEAD END. HM.
OOKAY... CAREFUL..
CAAREFULLL..
UHHH
WOBBLE
PHEW
KNOCK
THUNK
DSH!
SMASH
Z
Z Z
Z
Z Z

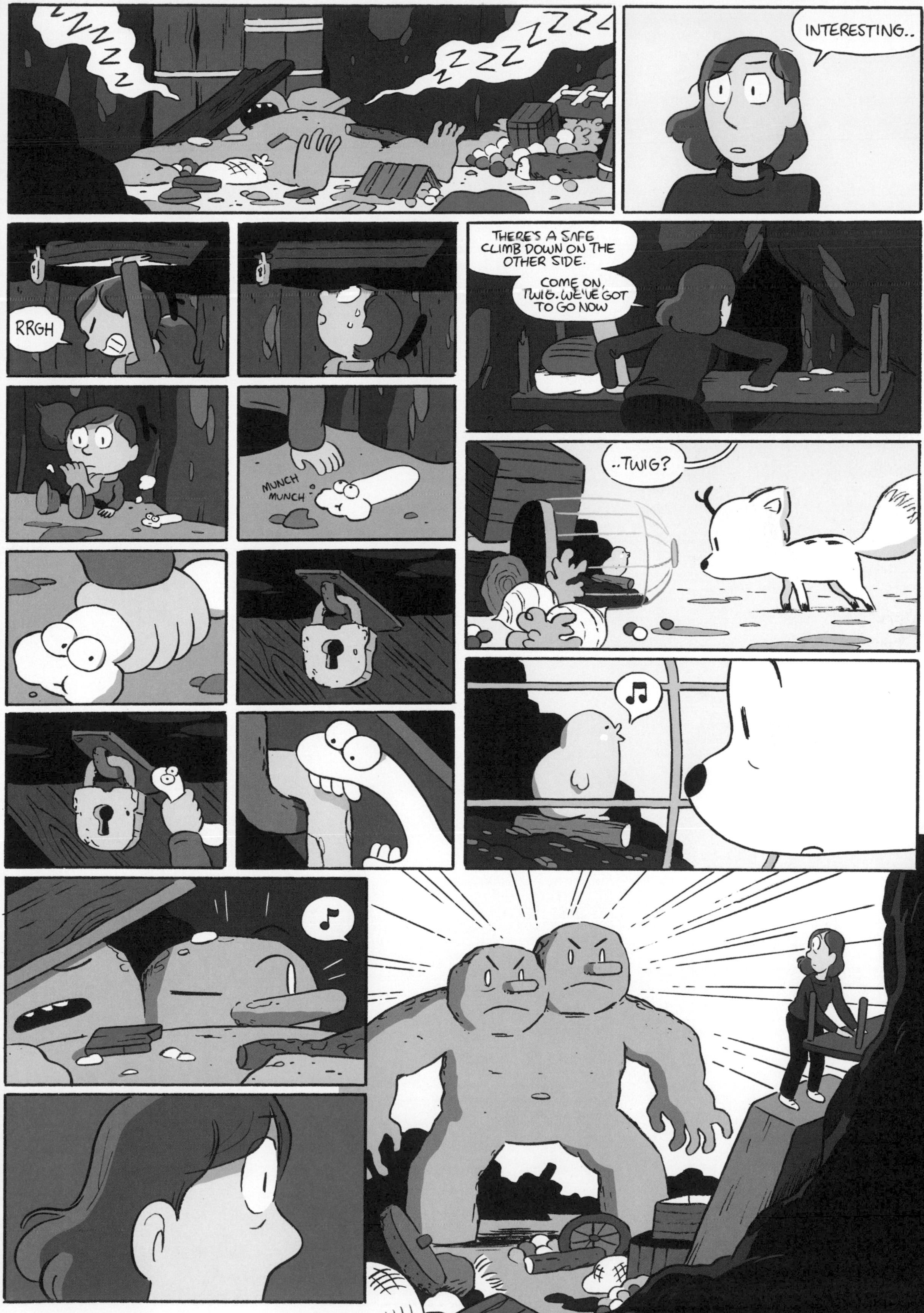

ZZZZZ
ZZZZZZZ
INTERESTING..
RRGH
THERE'S A SAFE CLIMB DOWN ON THE OTHER SIDE.
COME ON, TWIG. WE'VE GOT TO GO NOW
MUNCH MUNCH
..TWIG?

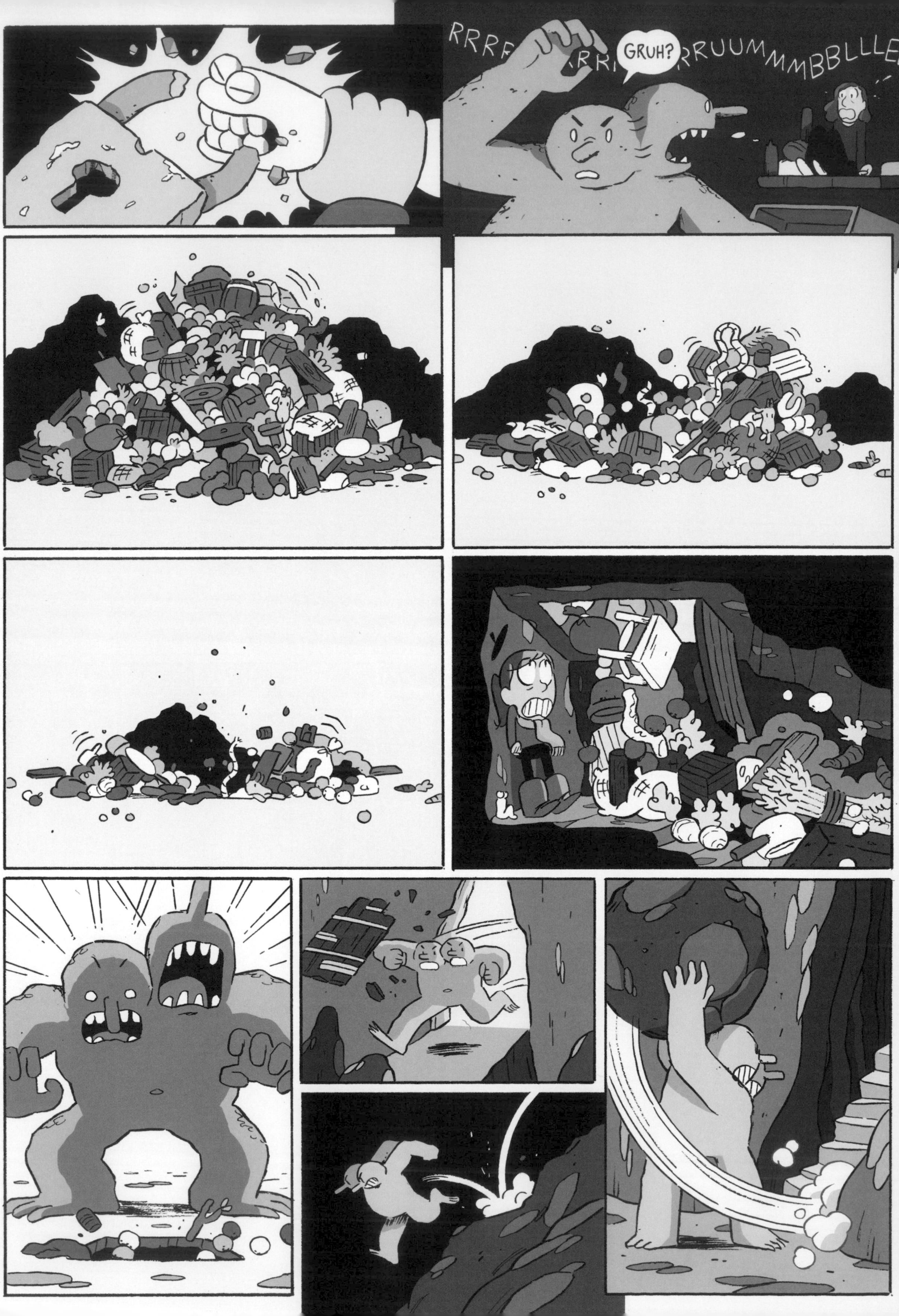
RRRR
RRR
GRUH?
RRUUMMMBBLLLE

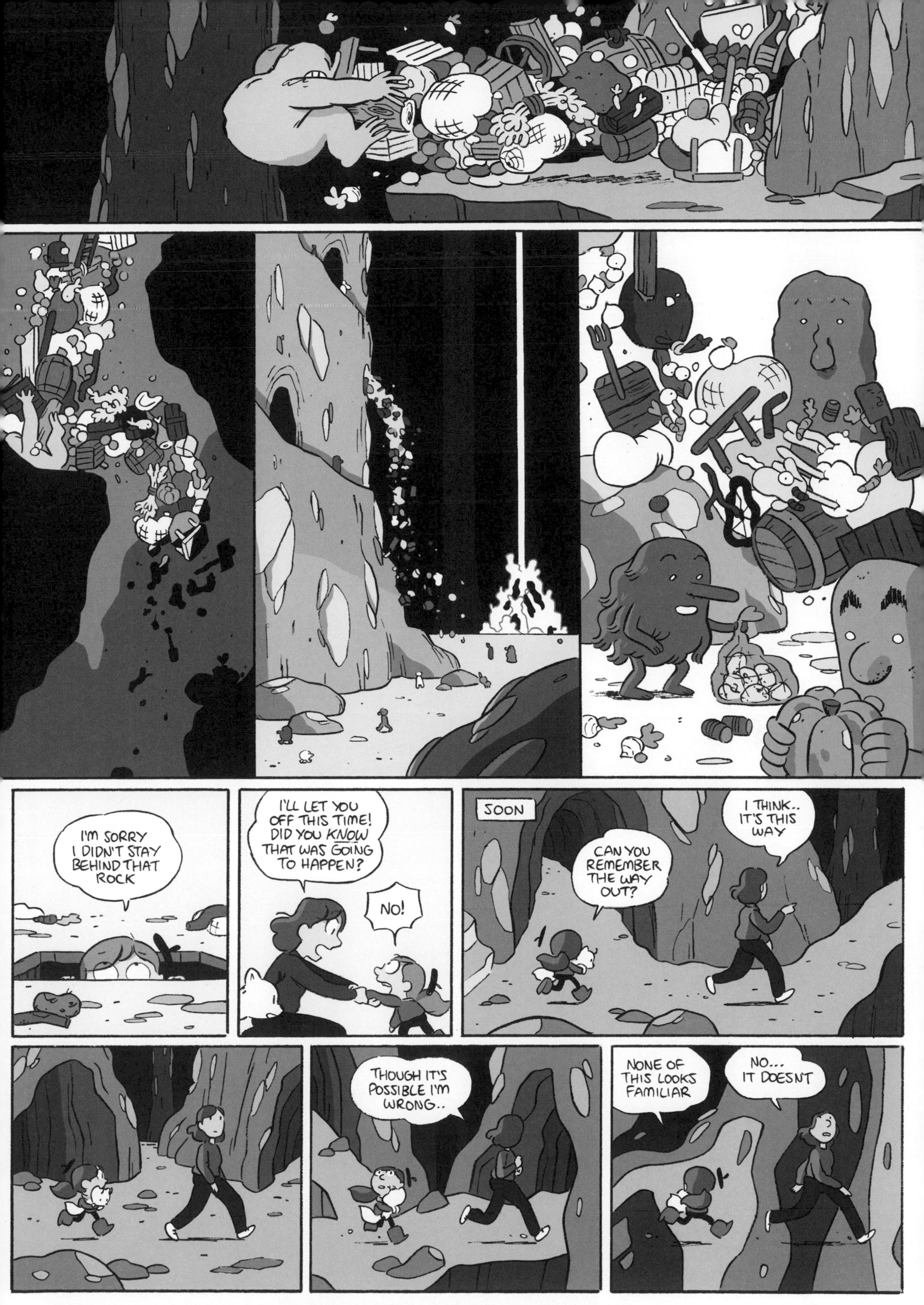
I'M SORRY I DIDN'T STAY BEHIND THAT ROCK
I'LL LET YOU OFF THIS TIME! DID YOU KNOW THAT WAS GOING TO HAPPEN?
NO!
SOON
CAN YOU REMEMBER THE WAY OUT?
I THINK.. IT'S THIS WAY
THOUGH IT'S POSSIBLE I'M WRONG..
NONE OF THIS LOOKS FAMILIAR
NO... IT DOESN'T

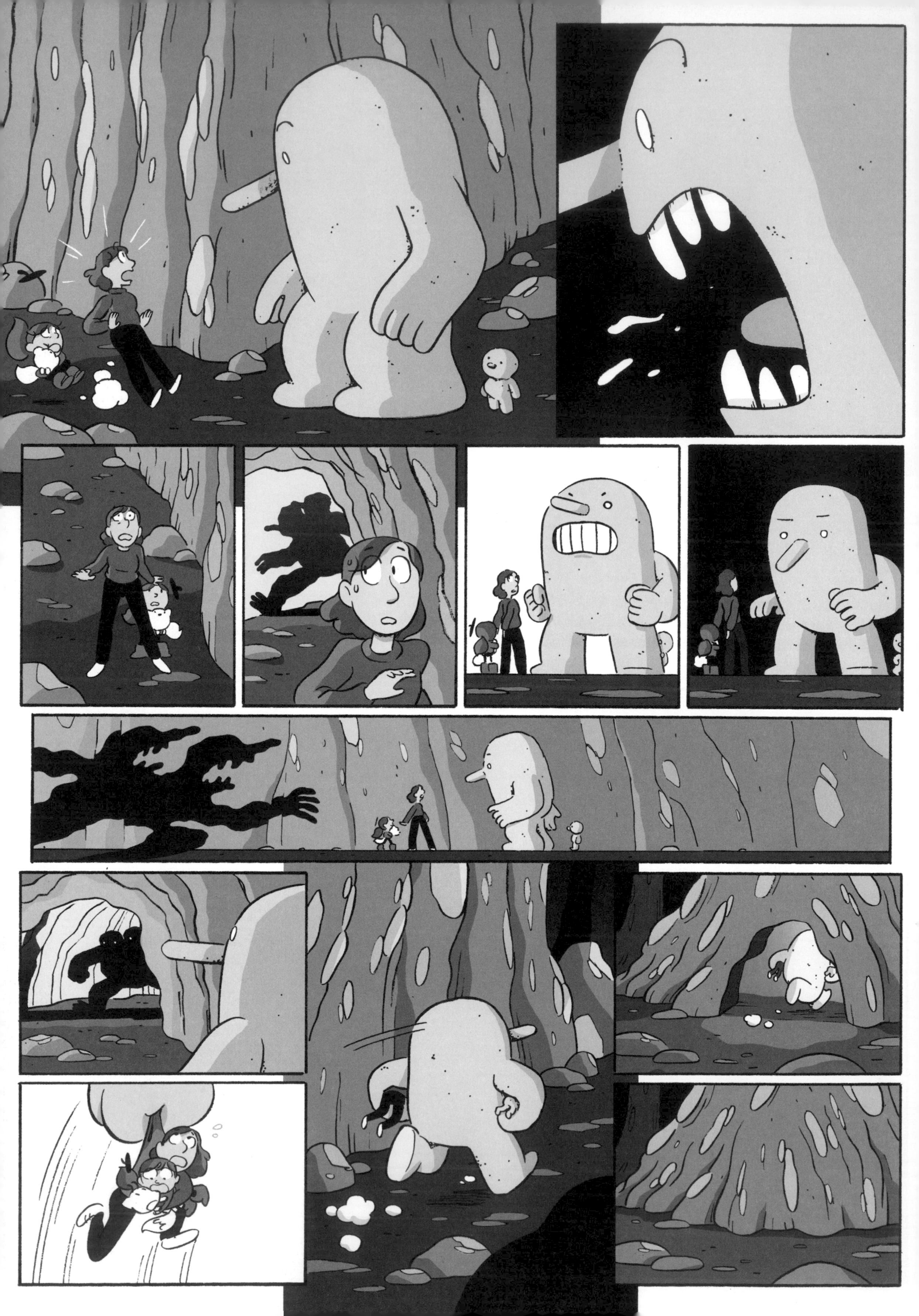

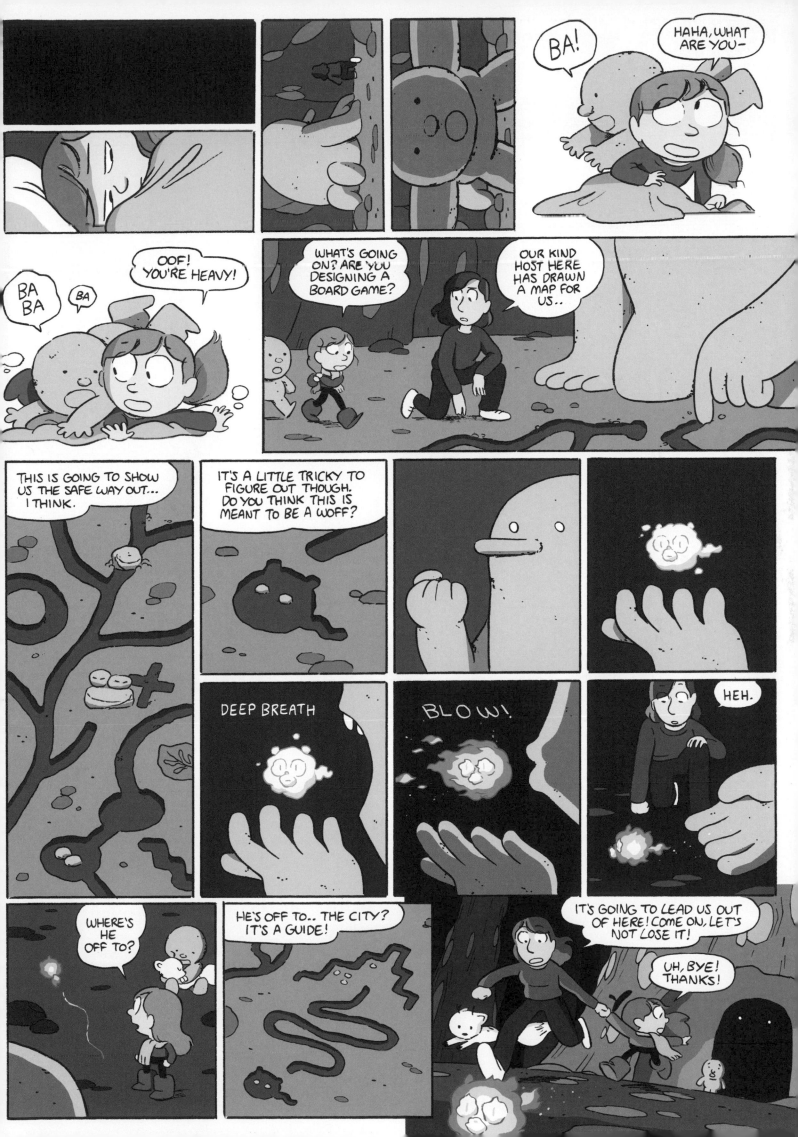

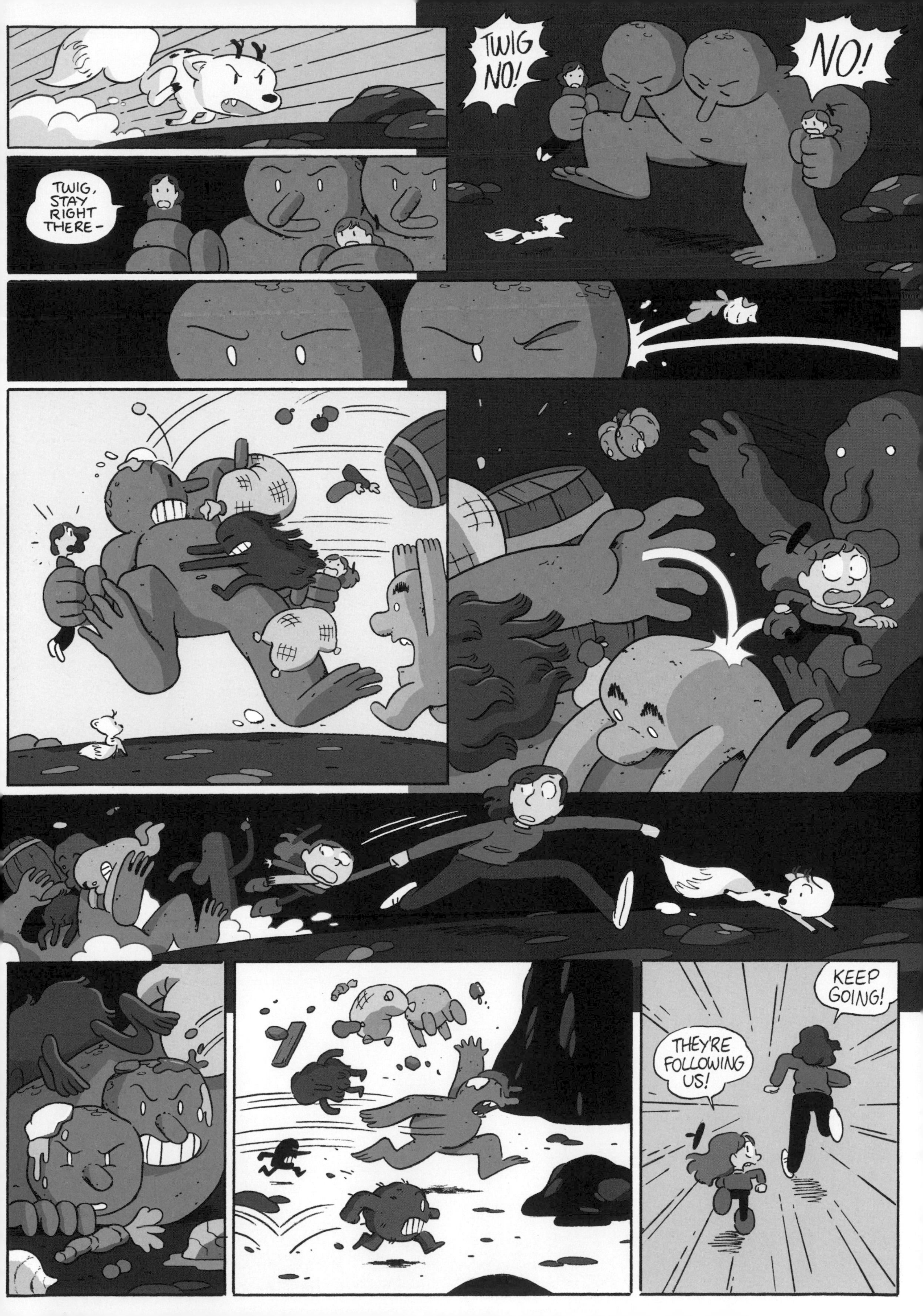
TWIG, STAY RIGHT THERE-
TWIG NO!
NO!
THEY'RE FOLLOWING US!
KEEP GOING!

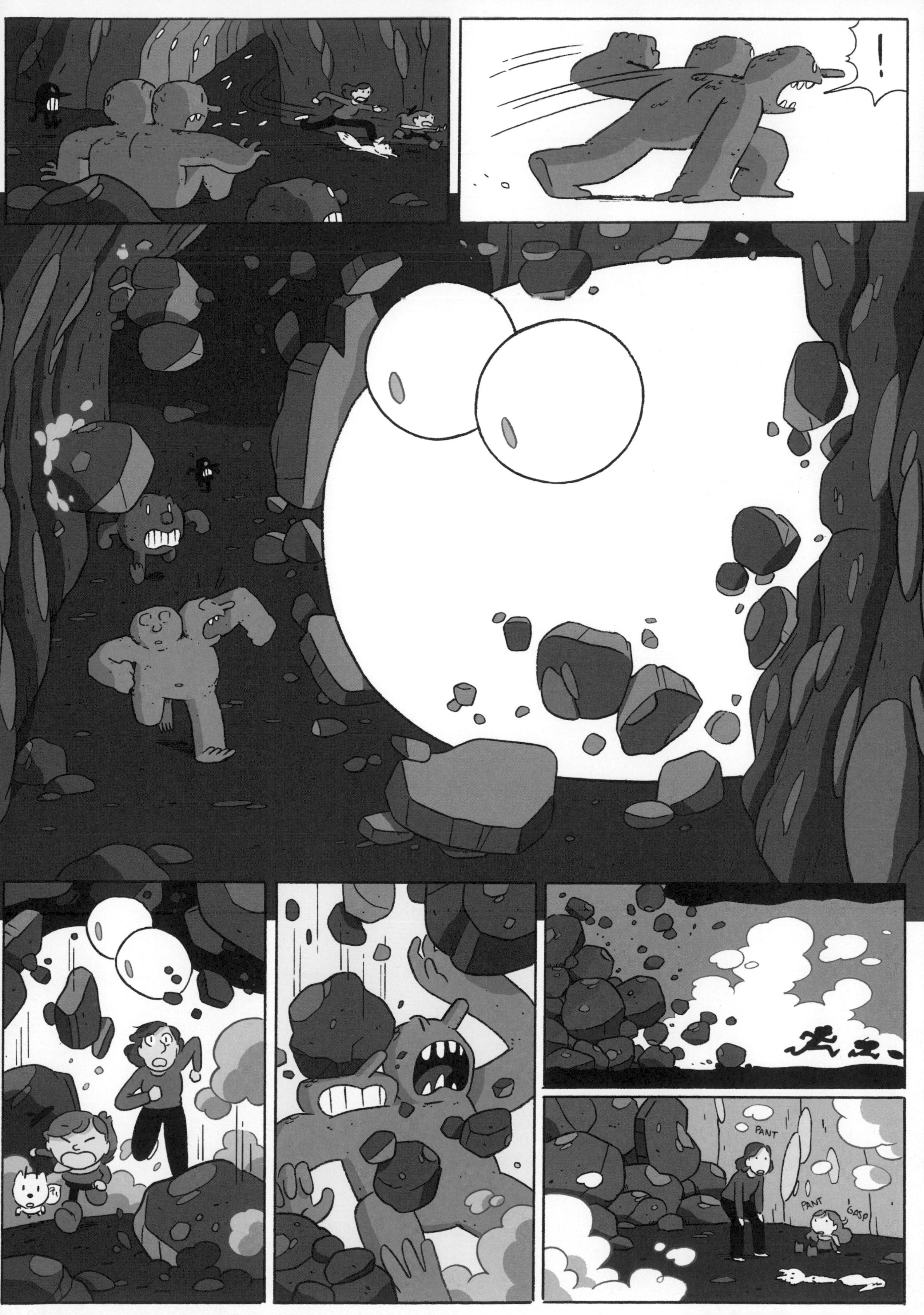
!
PANT
PANT
GASP

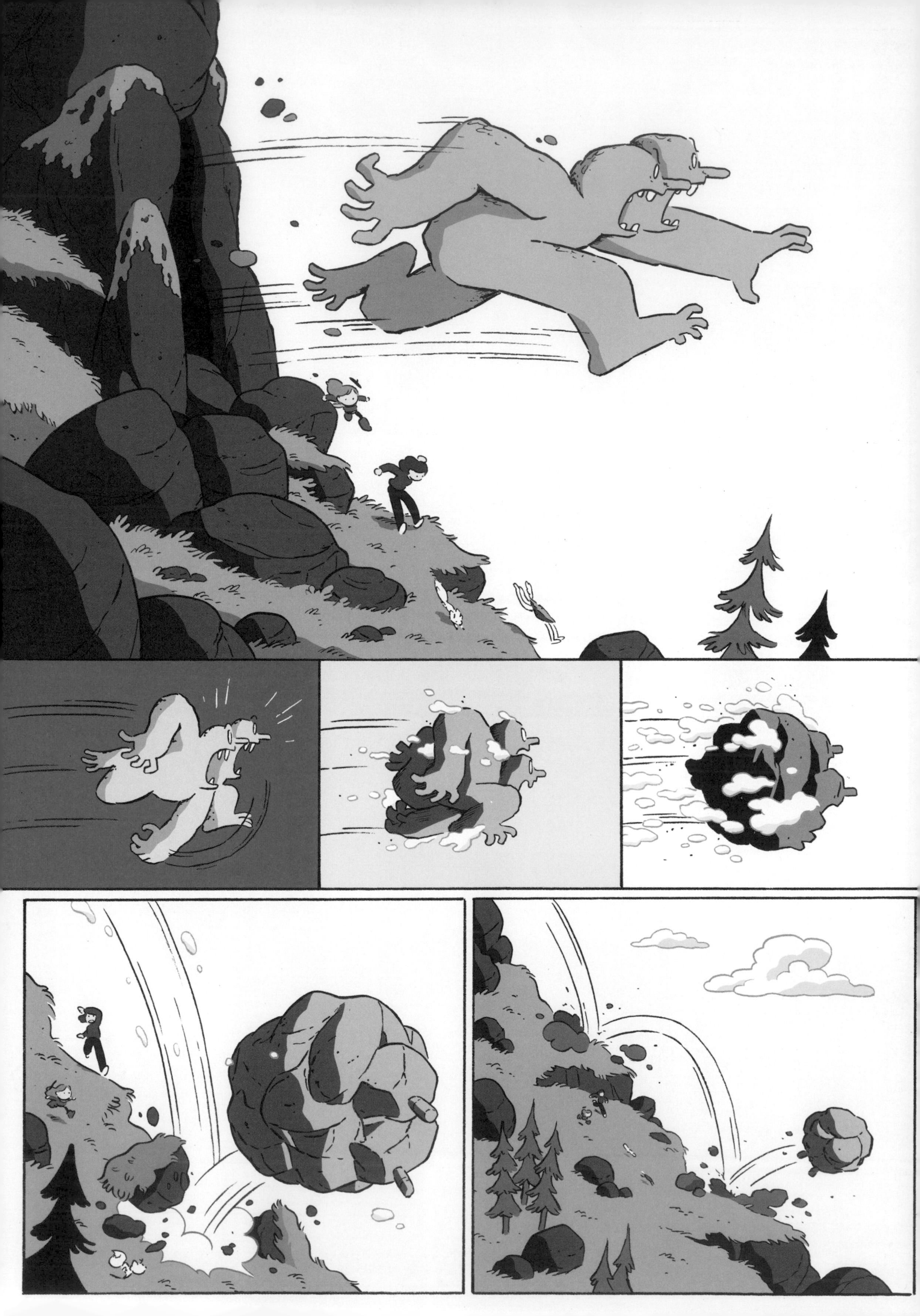

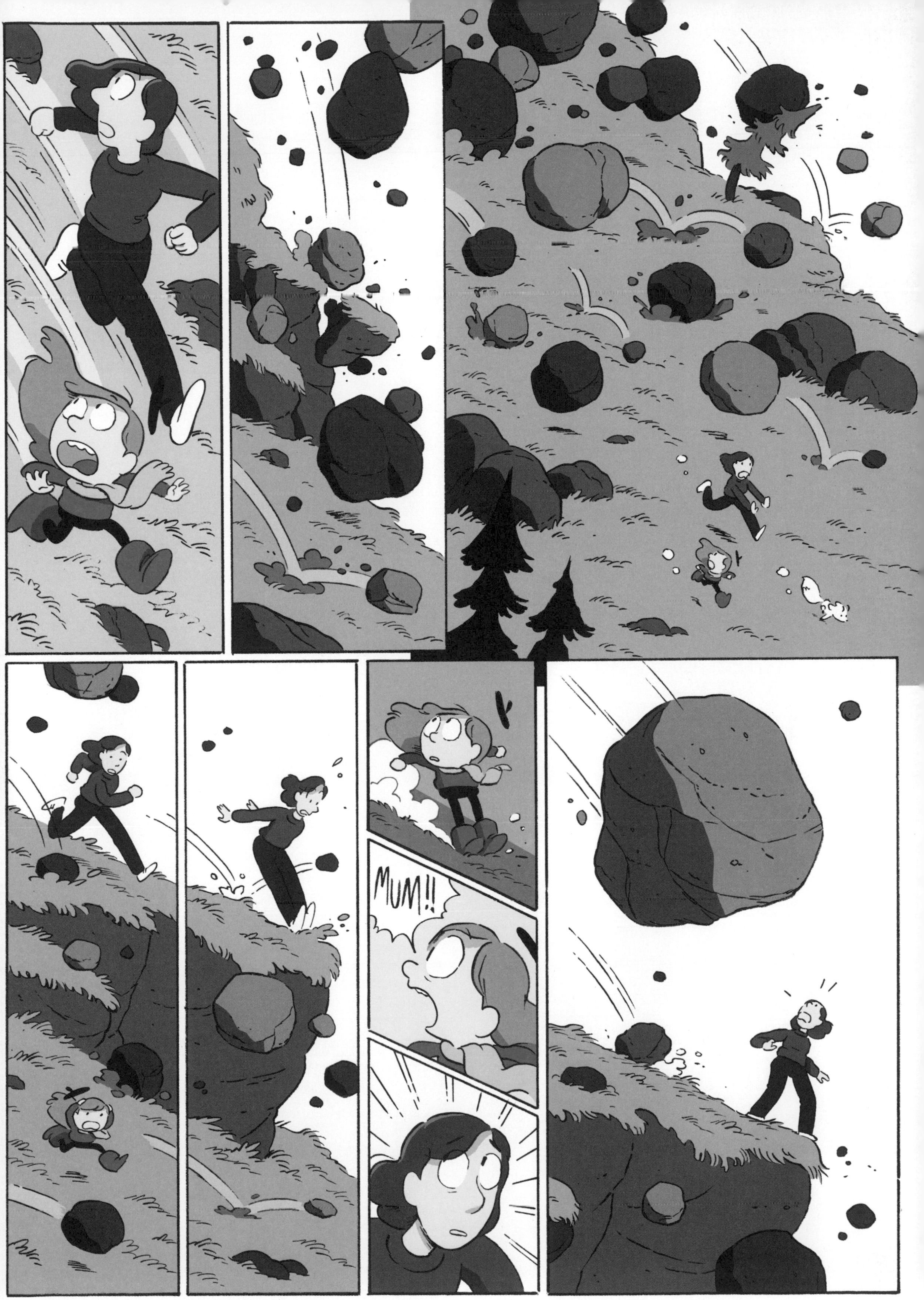
MUM!!

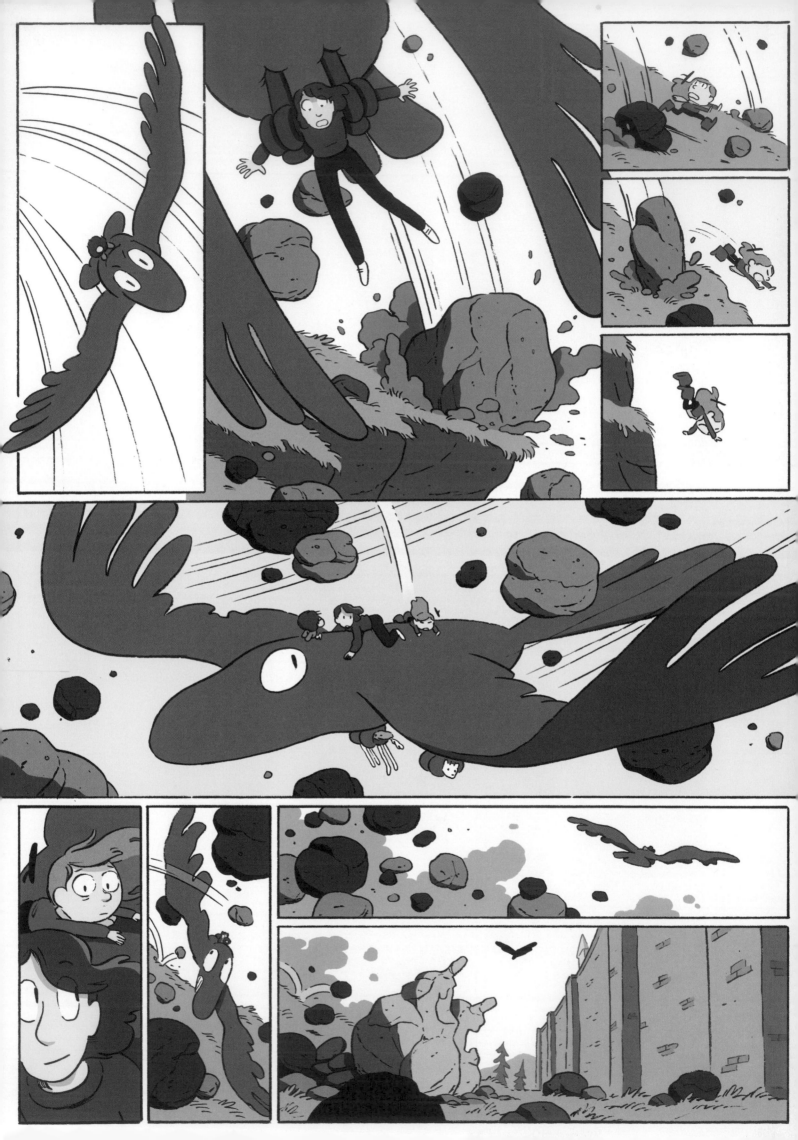

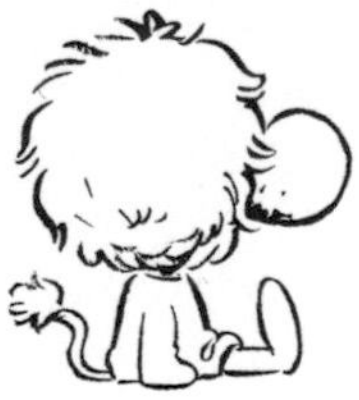

SPECIAL THANKS TO PHILIPPA RICE, EVERYONE AT NOBROW AND FLYING EYE, EM PARTRIDGE, JON MCNAUGHT, BJORN RUNE LIE, HANNA K, KURT MUELLER AND ALL MY FAMILY AND FRIENDS.

THIS IS A FIRST EDITION PUBLISHED IN 2016.

PUBLISHED BY FLYING EYE BOOKS, AN IMPRINT OF NOBROW LTD.
27 WESTGATE STREET, LONDON, E8 3RL
PUBLISHED IN THE US BY NOBROW (US) INC.

MIX
Paper from responsible sources
FSC® C002795

PRINTED IN LATVIA ON FSC ASSURED PAPER
ISBN 978-1-909263-74-1

ORDER FROM WWW.FLYINGEYEBOOKS.COM

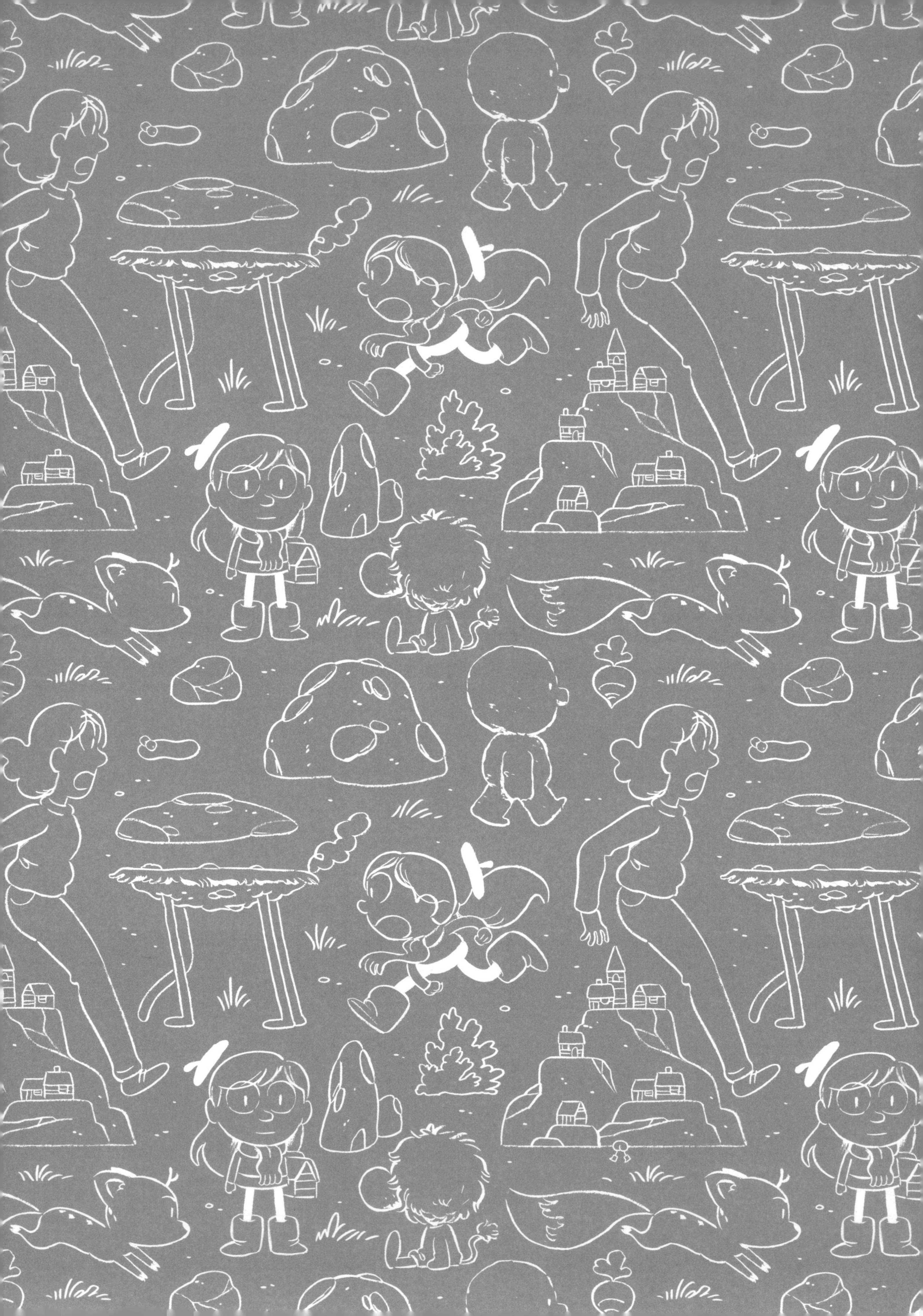